S0-BYU-991

Miss Ellie avoided Jock's piercing stare. She had never lied to him—not in all their years together—but this time it was necessary. Jock couldn't take the shock of knowing that two of his sons may have perished in a plane crash. And Ellie didn't dare say the awful words aloud . . . for fear they might be true.

———————————

Series Story Editor **Mary Ann Cooper** is America's foremost soap opera expert. She writes the nationally syndicated column *Speaking of Soaps*, is a contributor to leading soap opera magazines, and has appeared as a guest on numerous radio and television talk shows.

Writers **Paul Mantell** and **Avery Hart** are, between them, the authors of plays, children's records, educational cassettes, and humor articles. They live in New York City, but have come to think of Dallas as their second home.

Dear Friend,

Part of the success of the popular television series DALLAS lies in its ability to give the viewer an opportunity to be a bit of a snoop. Everyone is curious about what it's like to be rich and powerful. We all enjoy being the proverbial fly on the wall, privy to hidden family secrets, discovering where skeletons are buried.

This quirk of human nature seems to be most evident in times of great tragedy. In book 5 of the DALLAS series, the Ewing family is in the spotlight as they cope with the possible loss of Bobby and J.R. in a plane crash. You'll witness their mother's anguish and their wives' unspoken terror. For the first time you, as a reader, will be able to get inside the characters' heads and find out what motivates them. That's why Soaps & Serials paperback books are so special. As a reader, you have the opportunity to get to know your favorite daytime and nighttime characters. You may just be surprised at what you discover.

For Soaps & Serials books,

Mary Ann Cooper

Mary Ann Cooper

P.S. If you missed previous DALLAS books and can't find them in your local book source, please see the order form inserted in the back of this book.

DALLAS™

5

DANGEROUS DESIRE

From the television series created by David Jacobs

PIONEER COMMUNICATIONS NETWORK, INC.

Dangerous Desire

From the television series DALLAS™ created by David
Jacobs. This book is based on scripts written by D. C.
Fontana, Richard Fontana, and Leonard Katzman.

DALLAS™ paperback novels are published and
distributed by Pioneer Communications Network, Inc.

TM & Copyright © MCMLXXXVI by Lorimar
Productions, Inc. All rights reserved. Licensed by
Lorimar Licensing Co.

All rights reserved including the right to reproduce this
book or portions thereof in any form whatsoever. For
information write to: Pioneer Communications Network,
Inc., 825 Brook Street, Box 5006, Rocky Hill, CT 06067.

SOAPS & SERIALS™ is a trademark of Pioneer
Communications Network, Inc.

ISBN: 0-916217-85-X

Printed in the United States of America

10 9 8 7 6 5 4 3 2 1

5

DANGEROUS DESIRE

Chapter One

Pamela Barnes Ewing stared absently at the tall, graceful models twirling on stage. One after another, women of impossible beauty posed in front of her then disappeared, only to reappear minutes later in completely different outfits, equally alluring. She held her pad in her left hand, her pen in her right, but she had long since stopped taking notes. They had been in New York for only three days, but the buying trip had taken its toll on her. Since her arrival, she had seen nothing of New York except the suites and restaurants of the Waldorf-Astoria Hotel.

Pam was dismayed. The prospect of going to New York as temporary assistant buyer for The Store, the prestigious Dallas emporium where she worked, had been exciting, but the reality was completely disappointing to her. She missed her husband Bobby, who had gone off to New Orleans with his older brother J.R. in pursuit of a new construction deal.

It had been Pam's idea to take this job, and she had had to fight hard for it. Now she wondered if she'd done the right thing. After all, the Ewing family had so much money they didn't know what to do with it. Then she remembered how boring life had been for her hanging around Southfork, and how useless she had felt living totally off her husband's money with no life of her own apart from him. No, it was good that she had taken the job, no matter how tired she felt at the moment. Rubbing her face with her hands to get the blood running again, she picked up her pad and pen and once again began to pay attention to the job at hand.

Turning to the young designer next to her, she complimented him on his new designs, asking him some pertinent and flattering questions, such as how he had achieved a certain look and the color in one of the weaves. The designer grinned at her, pleased that she was impressed. The Store was a big potential customer for him. Despite Pamela Ewing's nominal position of assistant buyer, she was best friends with The Store's owner, Liz Craig, and a millionairess in her own right.

Liz herself made her way over to them. Her auburn hair was well styled and she wore an attractive yet businesslike dress. "The designs are wonderful, Davie," she gushed. "Now Pam, give me those numbers again." The designer tensed. The moment of truth was at hand. Liz Craig turned to him by way of explaining her hesitation, and said, "Have to make sure we don't order more than we can pay for."

Davie relaxed. The sale was made, and everything else was gravy. It had been a profitable day for him. Very profitable.

As Pam leafed through her notes, the phone rang. Still looking for the right figures, she went over to answer it. "Three dresses of every size, one gown each size and color," she shouted over to Liz as she picked up the receiver.

Liz smiled at Davie and made up her own mind based on Pam's calculations. "We'll take four of each dress, and two of each gown, for each store of course, but leave out the purple, will you? I can't stand it."

Davie laughed. "Liz," he moaned in exaggerated frustration, "are you aware that, in all the time I've known you, you've never ordered a single thing in purple? Now, I can understand if you don't like a certain color, but has it ever occurred to you that some of your customers might be wild about it? Everyone's tastes are different, you know."

Liz shook her head. "No purple, Davie. Everyone may have his own tastes, but in my store, what I say goes."

Pam returned. "Liz, that's the designer Pete Landers recommended. She wants to know where we are."

Liz blew out a long breath and thought for a minute before answering. "Tell her we'll be there in half an hour." Pam retreated to relay the message. "We've been running late ever since we got into town," Liz confided to Davie. "Do you realize we were supposed to be finished yesterday? We'll be lucky if we get out of town by midnight!" She laughed happily.

Liz Craig loved her work, and she especially loved buying trips. They afforded her the chance to travel, to wine and dine, and to buy the latest fashions for The Store. It was the most exciting part of an exciting career, and she found it hard to fathom why Pam had been so anxious to leave.

Pam had explained to her that she'd promised to meet Bobby in New Orleans, but she saw Bobby every day of her life! Here was her chance to meet new people, be on her own in a new city! Liz shook her head in puzzlement. Davie was right, apparently. Everybody's tastes were different. And Bobby was, after all, the most handsome man in Dallas.

At the phone, Pam repeated Liz's instructions, expanding the time allowed to give them room for error, using her own judgment and initiative as she knew Liz expected her to do. "We'll be over as soon as we can make it," she said, "figure about forty-five minutes, okay? Can you tell her that for me? Good. Bye, then." As she hung up the receiver, the light flashed on the phone indicating a caller on the other line. Pam depressed the button to take the call. "Hello?" she said, in her best business voice. But it was not a business call.

"Pammy?" said a distant voice on the other end of the line. It was Bobby.

"Hi, honey!" she said, as cheerfully as she could manage. She had let him down and she knew it. "I'm so sorry I couldn't get there last night . . . it's been crazy here. I did call . . . did you get my message?"

Bobby was peeved. She could tell by his voice, faint as it sounded.

"I got it, all right," he said tensely. "You know, Pam, we did plan this a long time ago. In fact, I went and reserved the same room we slept in the night we were married, as a surprise. Ha! Some surprise. The only surprise was sleeping in it alone."

Pam bit her lip. He was even angrier than she'd thought he would be, and he had every right to be. But what could she have done? She couldn't just walk off the job to be with him. She tried to soothe his hurt feelings, hard as that was to do over the telephone. "I'm really sorry, darling," she said softly, trying not to be overheard. "I'll tell you all about it when I see you. It's been really crazy here. Believe me, I feel as bad about this as you do. I really wanted to go to New Orleans and be with you . . ."

From the other end of the line came a snort of disbelief. "Did you really want to be with me, Pam? Not badly enough, apparently."

Bobby was being more difficult than she'd expected, and she didn't have time to talk to him now. "Bobby, try to understand," she whispered. "I have a job. I can't just walk off it anytime I feel like it. You know as well as I do that business sometimes gets in the way of a person's private life. How many times has the shoe been on the other foot?"

It was a good point, one that Bobby ordinarily would have seen the wisdom of, but right now he was hurt, and wasn't really listening. "What do I have to do to see more of my wife?" he complained. "Become a dress designer? Your job has been getting in the way of our private life an awful lot recently."

Now Pam was getting irritated. "They pay me, Bobby. They expect my time in return."

Bobby fumed. "If I want your time, how much do I have to pay to get it? Are you open to the highest bidder?" He was sorry he had said it as soon as the words escaped his lips.

On the other end of the line, Pam felt the sting of

his words. "We'll discuss it further when we get home," she said perfunctorily. "I'm in a meeting now, and they need me."

"Oh!" said Bobby, sarcastically. "So you are coming home. I was beginning to wonder."

Pam kept her cool, in spite of his harshness. "I love you, Bobby, whatever you may think of me. We'll be together again tomorrow, and we'll talk then. I have to go now. Bye." She hung up the phone feeling her insides spinning in turmoil. They would have to have some hard discussions when they got back home, and straighten out this whole issue. It had been a thorn in their relationship long enough.

On the other end of the line, Bobby stared at the receiver for a moment before hanging up. He swung open the door of the phone booth, and instantly the roar of airplane engines rose to greet him. He strode across the tarmac to the sleek Lear jet—the Ewing family's private plane. The noise and the wind of the airstrip swept away the anger and regret for the moment.

His brother J.R. was waiting for him on the tarmac, about halfway to the plane, his briefcase in hand and an impatient look on his face. Bobby had disappeared earlier that morning and had only shown up hours later, here at the airport. "Didn't I tell you I wanted to be at that meeting with you?" he demanded of Bobby. "I don't know what gets into you at times like this. That meeting with Cox was important, and I should have been there."

Bobby walked past him toward the plane. "My meeting with Cox concerned Ewing Construction. My company. There was no reason for you to be there. As I recall, you aren't all that hot on me being on my own in the first place, and I know what you think of construction as a business, too. Why in the world would I want to take you with me to that meeting?"

J.R. was furious. "Let me remind you of something, little brother. Your company is a subsidiary of Ewing Oil, which is our family business, the source of all our wealth and power, and the only reason you've got a construction business in the first place. I happen to be president of Ewing Oil. Our daddy has seen fit to place me in that position of trust. In a deal like this one, with over a million dollars at stake, there's every reason in the world for me to be there."

Bobby stopped and turned to him. "You're saying I can't handle big deals on my own?" he said.

"I'm saying I know you blew it," J.R. replied smugly.

J.R. had an amazing way of finding things out before anybody else did. How he could have known about Bobby's bid not being accepted was a mystery to Bobby, but he was not surprised that J.R. had managed to find out. It was par for the course. "I made Charlie Cox a good, fair bid on that condo deal," he began, but J.R. waved him off.

"Fair bid, my foot. If you think Cox'll accept an ordinary bid, you don't know him. He's a crook and a chiseler. He needs to be reminded that we hold the mortgage on his Fort Worth properties. Then he'll take any bid we offer him. And I'm going to remind him of that mortgage as soon as I get a chance."

Bobby was disgusted. J.R. made business

dealings seem like underworld machinations. "That's the only way you know, isn't it, J.R.?" he asked disdainfully. "Strong-arming, bullying, and coercing until you get what you want."

Bobby was hot, and oddly enough, it had the effect of calming J.R. down. It was almost as if, having angered his brother, J.R. could relax and be mature and level-headed about things. "Take it easy, boy," he said, smiling, "we're gonna get that deal, and that's what matters. How we get it is a minor matter."

They had reached the plane. From out of the cockpit jumped Johnnie, the Ewing family's longtime pilot. He was an experienced flyer, having flown combat missions in Vietnam, but his face belied his years and experience.

"Is everything ready, Johnnie?" J.R. wanted to know.

"Yes, sir, Mr. Ewing," the pilot replied politely. "But I've checked out the weather information, and there's a bad storm moving in pretty fast from the south. We might have a pretty bumpy ride back. I think we'd better lay over till it passes. Maybe by tomorrow morning it'll clear up enough to chance it," he explained with a shrug.

J.R. did not seem perturbed. "Come on, now, Johnnie," he chided, "we've gotten through these things lots of times before! You're not afraid, are you, boy? Come on, now, Vietnam must have been a lot worse than any storm's gonna be!"

Bobby noticed the pilot's discomfort. It was not Johnnie's place to contradict J.R., so Bobby thought he'd better intervene. "I think we ought to listen to Johnnie," he said.

But J.R., already exasperated by his brother's

incompetence with Charlie Cox, was not about to give Bobby a hearing in this small matter. "Maybe you've forgotten," he said, "about our meeting this afternoon with Ben Deering. Daddy wants us there, you know that. We can't let him down just 'cause of a bumpy flight." And, as if that settled it, he turned to the pilot and gave him instructions for the flight. "We'll divert north and fly around the edge of the weather. I want to be in the air in five minutes, Johnnie."

The pilot nodded, trying to dismiss his reservations. Reluctantly, he climbed into the cockpit and started up the engines.

J.R. began to follow the pilot up the steps but was stopped by Bobby, who grabbed him by the arm. "You're only happy when you're running things, aren't you? You always have to be the boss."

J.R. smiled indulgently. "My job is to be the boss, little brother," he said in a patronizing tone.

"Okay, J.R.," Bobby retorted, "we'll fly around the storm, but that's the end of it. From now on, you keep your nose out of Ewing Construction. Stick to your own turf at Ewing Oil, and keep out of my business."

It was a firm warning, but J.R. eluded its meaning, as if he could shake off such threats with impunity. "Bobby, you just don't know how to deal with people like Charlie Cox. I do."

"I'm well aware of your opinion regarding my abilities," Bobby shouted over the roar of the engines, "and I don't care what you think. Just keep your hands off my business, and keep your opinions to yourself!"

J.R. just smiled at his brother, his lip curling into a cruel smirk. "If you take care of your business like you take care of your little woman, Ewing Construction will be filing for Chapter Eleven before you know it."

Bobby felt as if he were about to explode with rage. Of course J.R. had known about Pam's expected arrival and about her failure to show up. J.R. hated Pam. She was a Barnes, one of the Ewings' hated enemies, and always would be so far as J.R. was concerned. Bobby felt an insane need to defend Pam from J.R.'s verbal assault, to defend himself from the charge of being ruled by his wife. It was an absurd charge. But the roar of the engines revving into high gear interrupted him, and he climbed into the cabin without another word. J.R. followed him in, and the two men took their seats as the plane swung into motion, lifting off into the darkening sky headed for Dallas.

Dr. Harlan Danvers looked like a cross between an old-fashioned country doctor and a successful neurosurgeon. In fact, he was both. He sat now in Jock Ewing's chair, at Jock Ewing's desk, making entries in Jock Ewing's medical portfolio. The patriarch of the Ewing clan paced restlessly up and down the floor as he buttoned up his shirt. He was a bundle of nervous energy, chomping at the bit, bucking like a bronco against the pull of his advancing age.

"Well, you old witch-doctor!" he bellowed affectionately at his old friend. "How long have I got? Five minutes?"

Danvers scowled. Some patients were more difficult, more intractable than others, and Jock Ewing was one of the worst. "Calling me names isn't going to help you, Jock. Sit down, if you want to hear your prognosis."

"I prefer to stand."

"Sit down!" shouted Danvers. Jock did so, grumbling all the while. Sometimes, reflected the doctor, you had to be cruel to do any good at all.

"I've been doing nothing but sitting and lying down for too long," complained Jock. "Standing feels good." Danvers ignored him, and finished writing down his notes. "Could you hurry it up, Harlan?" Jock pestered. "I got a lot of things to do, you know. I don't have time to sit around."

The doctor lifted his face to look at Jock. "It all depends on you just how much time you do have left, Jock," he said, meaningfully.

"And just what is that supposed to mean?" Jock wanted to know.

"Well, for one thing," answered the other man, "it means you'll probably live longer than you've got a right to, longer than you deserve, you old coot." Jock smiled. "But remember," the doctor cautioned him, "you've just had a triple bypass. That's a serious operation. I want you to take it easy, you understand? You can't run all over the place anymore, not if you expect to live a full life."

"Now wait a minute!" shouted Jock. "I've got a ranch to run here! You don't think I'm gonna let it all go to hell, do you?"

"That's what you've got a foreman for," Danvers said. "You want to help out a little, okay. But don't go doing everything yourself, you hear?"

Jock was so disgusted that he felt like spitting. The whole point of the doctor's visit was supposed to have been to give him a clean bill of health, so he could put aside all this laziness and get back to living. "I don't know why I allow you to come over here and scrutinize every last inch of me," he groused.

"I don't know why I even came," shot back the doctor. "You sure aren't any fun to have as a patient, you know. And this is the only house call I make. I don't have to do those kinds of things anymore. Count yourself lucky. And either you do what I say, or you find somebody else whose advice is more to your liking. But I don't think you'll find anyone like that in a hurry."

Jock smiled. He and Harlan Danvers went back many years, and the doctor had saved his life on the operating table not six months ago.

"So," said Danvers, "will you do as I say, and take it easy?"

Jock pretended to ruminate over it for a moment. "I'll think about it." Then he laughed a broad laugh, and the doctor, having gotten his message across, laughed with him.

Finally alone in their suite, Pam and Liz were able to take their shoes off and relax. Liz was exultant, and her tiredness was sheer pleasure, the reward of abundant and fruitful work. For Pam, her weariness had as much to do with the ambivalance over this whole trip, and indeed, her whole brief career. Her mind was on Bobby, angry at him, missing him, preoccupied with him.

"Boy oh boy," laughed Liz, "that was some morning! I hope things go more smoothly from here on in!" It wasn't so much a complaint as a congratulation to the woman who had shared the trip with her. "Hey Pam," she went on, "how 'bout an expensive lunch, a massage and a sauna before dinner? We're seeing Josh Morgan, and I think we deserve to look and feel our best!"

Normally Pam would have jumped at the prospect, but today was different. She hesitated for a moment before saying, "Y'know, Liz, I was thinking of leaving right now for Dallas. I could hop an early afternoon flight . . ." She looked up at Liz with a pleading gaze.

"Miss him, do you?" Her boss smiled wryly. Pam nodded. She was hopelessly in love with her husband. Suddenly Liz felt a pang of envy for her friend's good fortune. Rich and in love—what could be better? But it was only for a moment. Liz Craig loved her life and wouldn't have traded it for anything. "You sure, Pam? Josh Morgan's an important contact—top publicity man and all . . ." She could see that Pam was not impressed by Josh Morgan, or at least, had not changed her mind about going home early. "Oh, go ahead." She grinned. "That husband of yours is pretty cute. If he was mine, I might skip out myself."

Pam smiled, and reached for the phone.

On the other end of the line was Lucy Ewing, Pam's niece. She had a guitar in her hand on which she'd been practicing. Her current ambition was to be a singer, and all her free time was spent in pursuit of that goal. Lucy took the message, promising to convey it to Bobby as soon as he and J.R. got home.

As she hung up, Jock entered the room with Miss Ellie, Lucy's grandmother. They were not a little surprised to see their granddaughter at home in the middle of a school day. "You have an explanation, I suppose," demanded Jock.

"Why, yes I do, Granddaddy," said Lucy, who

had always had her grandparents wrapped around her little finger. Jock and J.R. had practically driven her father away, and her mother too. The Ewings had brought Lucy up to be one of them, but, because of the guilt surrounding the circumstances of her youth, Lucy held the upper hand on all minor matters at Southfork. "I only had study hall this morning," she lied, "and I figured I could study just as well at home." Not waiting for the obvious absurdity of this answer to sink in, she changed the subject. "That was Pam," she said brightly. "She's on her way home from New York . . . flight 401 at three-thirty. She asked if Bobby could pick her up."

Jock looked puzzled. "Wasn't she supposed to join Bobby in New Orleans and fly back with the boys?" He looked at his wife.

Miss Ellie, in her infinite wisdom, knew it was best to keep her nose out of her children's private quarrels. "People have been known to change their plans, Jock," she said, patting his arm.

Jock drew away from her touch, unsatisfied with her answer. "This used to be an orderly family. Lately, I don't know where anyone is half the time." He strode off, disturbed at the trouble brewing in his house.

Cliff Barnes sat in his law office clearing up old business. During his recent run for the state senate he had let his law practice lie fallow. But now the campaign was over, the election lost, thanks to J.R. Ewing's smear tactics, and there were bills to pay. He would never think of asking his sister Pam for money, even though he knew she had more than enough. The thought of being beholden to Bobby

Ewing was more than he could bear. His father had allowed himself to get into debt to Jock Ewing, and had wound up a drunken bum. Cliff had sworn to himself that he would avenge his father, but incurring another debt from the Ewings wasn't the way to do that. No, there were other ways. He had only to wait, and opportunities would surely come his way.

He was reading through a contract, making notes on a legal pad, when the intercom buzzed. It seemed he had a visitor, and not just an ordinary visitor, either. It was Sue Ellen Ewing, J.R.'s wife. Cliff wondered why she had come to see him.

"Show her into my office," he told the secretary. He turned to the mirror for a quick look, then turned and smiled at his visitor as she came shyly through the door. She was radiantly beautiful, as a former Miss Texas ought to be, and the blush on her cheeks only served to accentuate her beauty.

"You must be surprised to see me here," she began, awkwardly.

"That's putting it mildly," Cliff admitted.

"I have a favor to ask of you . . ." she began.

Cliff laughed silently, bitterly. The nerve of the Ewings! To come and ask favors from him—after all that had just happened!

But Sue Ellen continued. "I know it must sound absurd, considering what you've just been through because of our family, but I had to see somebody about this and there's no one else I know who I can trust. You see, J.R. has spies everywhere. I figured you're one person who wouldn't run and tell him. When I tell you what I've come for, I think you might consider helping me."

Cliff looked at her skeptically. What could he

possibly be willing to do for her?

"I can pay you well, of course," she added.

"All right, Mrs. Ewing, why don't you get on with it and tell me what it is you want!"

She sat down in the armchair facing his desk, a client now, speaking with her attorney. "A couple of months back, you may recall, you ran into me when I was having a meeting with an attorney named Buzz Connors . . ."

Cliff nodded. He remembered thinking, *What's someone like Sue Ellen Ewing doing consulting with a crook lawyer like Buzz Connors?*

"Well," confided Sue Ellen, "I was meeting with him to try to adopt a baby."

Cliff emitted a low whistle. It was not what he had expected to hear. He knew, through Pam, about J.R. and Sue Ellen's vain efforts to have a child and the fact that they'd been trying for seven years, but still—adoption! It didn't sound like something J.R. would go for. "Your husband agreed to adopt a baby?" he asked incredulously.

Sue Ellen shook her head quickly. "That's just the point," she said. "He was against it, and when he learned about it he flew through the roof. He forced Rita Briggs, the child's natural mother, to leave town. I have no idea where she went, and J.R. isn't about to tell me. That's why I'm here." She looked him straight in the eye. "I want you to get me that baby, in spite of my husband."

Cliff scowled. He would have liked to help her, but how could he? The law was the law. "I'd like to give J.R. a kick in the rear like that, Mrs. Ewing, I really would. But there's no way, I'm afraid." Seeing that Sue Ellen was about to plead with him, he continued quickly, explaining his refusal. "You see, it's not a question of ethics. It's purely a practical matter. Say I found the girl for you. There's still no chance of your being able to adopt the baby without your husband's expressed consent. That's the law, Mrs. Ewing. I'm sorry."

Sue Ellen was on the verge of tears. "There must be some way around the law . . ." she protested meekly, hopelessly.

Cliff shook his head. "I'm afraid there isn't. You could divorce your husband, of course. That would make it possible. But you're not prepared to do that. Are you, Mrs. Ewing?"

Sue Ellen hesitated. In that moment she would have liked to do just that; to deal the mighty J.R. a blow he would never forget, to pay him back for all his infidelities, all his lying. But there was too much at stake for her. The Ewing name and privileges were very important to her. "No, I'm not," she replied softly.

Cliff looked at the woman seated across from him. He felt genuinely sorry for her. Being married to J.R. Ewing must be hell, especially for a soft, vulnerable creature such as Sue Ellen. He felt genuine affection for this woman who was the wife of his enemy. "I really am sorry," he said.

She shrugged her shoulders, fighting bravely to keep back the tears. "I didn't hold out much hope," she whispered. "But still, I thought that, somehow, there'd be a way . . ." Her voice faded, despair overwhelming her.

Cliff felt his heart go out to her. "Hey," he said, chiding, "How's about you let me take you to lunch?" She stared up at him. "Mrs. Ewing, consider the enormity of the offer. I *never* buy lunch—for *anybody*!"

Sue Ellen laughed in spite of herself. Cliff had won her over, his cheerfulness infecting her mood. She smiled weakly, but warmly, and allowed him to lead her out of the office, his arm around her.

The small jet bounced up and down erratically as it pierced heavier and heavier layers of clouds. The sky outside grew darker every minute as Johnnie raced northward, trying to skirt the storm. Inside the cabin, Bobby and J.R. sat grimly across from one another, trying to brace themselves as best they could against the jolts the plane was taking. Bobby stared angrily out of the window, the skies matching his mood. He was still bristling from his argument with his brother.

"I guess you intend to stare out the window like a dummy this whole trip long," J.R. said off-handedly.

"It's all I can see any point in doing," his brother replied, without taking his eyes off the window. "The two of us just don't seem able to speak to each other for more than a minute without getting into an argument about something or other."

"I'm aware of that, Bob," said his older brother. "But we're gonna have to remedy that."

Bobby looked at him. "And how do you propose to do that?" he asked.

"We just have to learn to have faith in one another . . ."

Bobby couldn't believe his ears. Was his brother really saying what he thought he said?

But J.R. finished his sentence, clearing up Bobby's confusion, ". . . so you don't feel it necessary to go off secretly to important business meetings without bringing me along."

"Or vice-versa?" Bobby inquired pointedly.

In a moment, hail began pounding the wing, drawing their attention away from each other. The plane rocked more precipitously than before. It gave a sickening lurch downward, then just as suddenly it came up again.

"I guess it's going to be a little rougher than I had thought," J.R. admitted.

They got up without another word and gingerly made their way to the cockpit to confer with Johnnie. Outside, lightning flashed everywhere as the hail continued to pound the plane and the winds increased, rocking it to and fro.

Just as the two of them reached the cockpit, there was a brilliant flash, and the main electrical system began shooting out sparks from the control panel. Small fires began breaking out everywhere in the cockpit.

"What's going on?" J.R. shouted over the noise.

"We've lost our whole electrical system!" shouted the pilot. "We're losing power fast!"

J.R. looked at his brother, his mind working quickly. "Can we get off a call for help?" he shouted to the pilot.

Johnnie shook his head. "Everything's dead."

Bobby grabbed a fire extinguisher and started spraying the flames. "The airport still has us on their radar," he said, offering a bit of consolation. But just then the plane veered out of control completely and began to plummet.

"Hold on tight!" screamed Johnnie as the plane went into a steep dive.

They all stood upright, bracing their hands against the sides of the cockpit. Stark, gripping fear darkened their faces. The deafening noise of the plane shrieked in their ears as their lives flashed before them. Then there was a loud explosion as the plane hit the ground, and everything went black.

Chapter Two

In the huge, warmly furnished room that served as the Ewing family study, Miss Ellie sat, writing some letters, catching up on her correspondence. She hardly looked up when the phone rang on her desk. Reaching for it with her left hand as she signed the letter she had just finished, she crooked the phone against her ear. "Hello?"

It was Bert, the Ewing family mechanic. He wanted to speak to Jock.

"My husband is resting upstairs right now, Bert. No, I can't disturb him . . . doctor's orders. What seems to be the trouble?"

Bert was agitated, but tried to remain calm, marshalling his resources for the shock he was about to administer. "Well, ma'am," he said with a slight stammer. "Air Traffic Control just got in touch with us here at the airport. Apparently, our plane disappeared from their screens a little while ago in the vicinity of Cado Swamp."

Miss Ellie felt herself swoon and grabbed the

desk in front of her for support, her heart pounding in fear. "Tell me everything," she demanded.

"Well," the mechanic replied, "we don't know much just yet. Everything was all right last time they called in. But there's a storm cutting through the area on their flight plan, and apparently it's a pretty bad one."

Miss Ellie's mind raced like a whirlwind. Perhaps they had merely made an emergency landing. There were a hundred explanations. It was no time to panic. "Bert," she said coolly into the phone, "listen to me. I want you to get all the information you can. Also, phone Earl McCrady at the Department of Public Safety. I want a search initiated as soon as he can get helicopters in the air. Tell him *I* said so." Years of being Dallas' premiere hostess and community service leader had provided Miss Ellie with connections in all the right places. Now was the time to use them. "I'll get back to you in a little while. Now get this straight. No one is to call here. No one. And my husband is to know nothing about this. Do you understand, Bert?"

Bert acknowledged her instructions, and she hung up the phone. Suddenly all the strength she had gathered for the moment left her body, and she swayed in fear and worry. But it was only for a moment. Miss Ellie was made of strong stuff. She pulled herself together quickly, rose from the desk, and hurried out the door. There were things to be done.

Ray Krebbs, foreman of Southfork Ranch, listened soberly as Miss Ellie told him the news. Lucy sat next to him, stunned into silence. The living room looked huge and empty. Ray shuddered as he realized that its emptiness might now be permanent. "Does Jock know anything about this yet?" he asked Miss Ellie.

She shook her head in response. "He doesn't, and I don't want him to, either," she said. "We don't know what happened yet, and until we do . . ." she paused for a moment, keeping the dark thoughts at bay, "no one's going to say a word about it."

Ray was dubious. Jock was, after all, the master of the house and the head of the family. "Gee, ma'am," he said, doubtfully, "I don't know if we should . . ."

Miss Ellie stopped him in his tracks. "The news could kill him, Ray. We can't chance that." There was no arguing the point.

Lucy seemed to have come out of her frozen state. "It's just so incredible!" she whispered.

"Now, Lucy," Miss Ellie said, putting her arm around the girl, "they may be all right. We'll just have to wait and see, and hope."

Ray rose and started for the door, putting on his hat. "Well," he said, "if I expect to be at the airport to meet Pam's plane, I'd better be on my way." He paused for a moment, visualizing Pam's reaction. "It's going to be awful hard for her to take," he added.

Miss Ellie knew it was true, but that did not change her resolve. "I know, Ray," she said, "but by the time she comes through that door . . ." she pointed to the front door of the mansion, "she's going to pretend he's just a few minutes late for dinner, do you understand? I may have lost Bobby and J.R., but I'll be damned if I'm going to lose Jock too," she vowed.

Ray looked at Miss Ellie, her face gray, ashen with grief, but firm with determination. He nodded in assent and continued toward the door. Lucy jumped up. She dreaded sitting around waiting for news to come in and having to pretend for Jock's sake. "I guess I'll go try to find Sue Ellen, okay, Grandma?"

But Ellie shook her head. "No, Lucy, I'll do that myself. I don't have the slightest idea where she could have gone off to today . . ." She reached for the phone, putting an end to the discussion. It seemed that Miss Ellie, too, needed to occupy herself.

Lucy ran out the door, catching up with Ray outside. He stood beside the Ewing company car, the keys in his hand. Lucy put her hand on the door handle to stop him from opening it. "Ray," she said, in a hushed voice, "what are you going to say to her?"

He stared into the distance. "I don't have the faintest idea, Lucy. What can I say? That it looks like Bobby's dead?" He shook his head, perplexed. "I'll figure out something on the way to the airport, I guess."

She put her hand on his shoulder. "Let me come with you, Ray. I'll tell her."

Ray looked at the young girl in front of him, who had had so many troubles already in her short life. It was tempting for him to shift the burden of bearing bad news to her shoulders. But in the end he couldn't do it. It was something that had been entrusted to him to do, and he had to face up to the task. "No, that's all right, Lucy, I'd better go myself," he answered. "Your grandma might be needing you. You never know."

As he drove away, the car kicking up a cloud of dust as it gathered speed, Lucy stood there, alone in the vast landscape, feeling completely lost, completely useless.

Ray paced back and forth in the waiting area watching the passengers disembark from the plane. He craned his neck, searching for the sight of Pam coming down the tunnel, but, she was one of the last to get off. His discomfort mounted with each passing moment. This was going to be one of the hardest things he had ever had to do in his life.

Finally, after what seemed an eternity of waiting, he saw her familiar form coming toward him, a spring in her step and a smile on her face, obviously glad to be home. When she saw Ray, surprise registered in her eyes for a moment. She had expected to see Bobby. But her smile quickly reappeared, answered by the best smile Ray could muster. Inside he was squirming. This was going to be even more difficult than he had imagined.

"Hi Ray." She waved as she approached him. "Things must be pretty quiet on the ranch for you to be able to take the afternoon off and come get me!"

Ray nervously rubbed his chin with his hand. "To tell you the truth, Pam, we're pretty busy. There's a big cattle auction next week . . . but I managed to get away . . . uh, you have any other bags?"

She handed him a ticket. "One more," she replied.

Ray nodded, and, motioning with his hand for her to stay where she was, he went over to the phone bank and made a quick call. When he returned, he said, "One of the hands will come by later and pick it up and bring it home. Let's go, now."

As he turned away, Pam, sensing something amiss, grabbed him by the arm. "What's going on here, Ray? Is something wrong? It's not Jock, is it?" Her father-in-law's delicate health was the first explanation that came to mind, but Ray shook his head.

"Jock's just fine, Pam." Then he sighed, and, taking her by the hand, he guided her over to a corner, out of earshot of any passers-by.

"Well, what is it, then, Ray? If Jock's okay, what's going on?"

Again Ray rubbed his chin, increasingly uncomfortable. This was going to hurt. "Miss Ellie sent me to pick you up, because . . . and to tell you that . . ." He looked at her hopelessly, unable to continue for the moment.

Pam's intuitive mind suddenly pieced together what he was trying to say. "It isn't Bobby, is it? Oh, Ray, don't tell me it's Bobby!"

Ray quickly put his arm around her, to support her. The gesture was confirmation of her worst fears. In order to soften the blow, he couched his words in the most optimistic way possible. "Well, nothing's for sure yet, Pam. We just don't know, but the plane went down in a storm. They're already searching for J.R. and Bobby. That's all there is to tell right now . . . but they'll find them . . . they'll find them."

Pam felt the panic rising in her chest like a train coming down the tracks headed right for her. Her whole life was blowing up in her face—everything might be gone! She had to know . . . she had to help, somehow . . . Bobby might still be alive, somewhere . . . he might need help! She had to do something! "Ray," she said, steadying herself for the emergency at hand, "take me to the search headquarters. I want to help. Maybe they'll let us join the search . . ."

Ray interrupted her lest she get so carried away that she couldn't be brought back down to earth. "Pam, there's nothing we can do that isn't being done already, believe me . . . come on now, Miss Ellie's expecting us back home. We're already late. She may have heard something by now. Oh, and listen. She doesn't want Jock to know anything. She's afraid the shock might kill him. Everybody— Sue Ellen, Lucy, you, me—we're all going to act like nothing's happened."

Pam was dumbfounded. "What are you talking about, Ray? You can't hide something like this! That's crazy!"

Ray shrugged helplessly. "Those are Miss Ellie's orders, Pam. Maybe it is crazy, but she's counting on all of us to keep it from him until we know . . . one way or the other."

Pam breathed deeply, the reality of the situation just beginning to sink in. "I don't think I can do that good an acting job, Ray . . . I really don't." But she knew she was going to try. What else was there for her to do? She had to keep a lid on her feelings anyway, until they knew for sure. She swallowed hard, pushing down the scream that welled up in her chest.

Ray hugged her. "There's still hope, Pam," he reassured her. "We've got to hang on to that." Taking her by the arm, his other arm around her shoulder for support, he led her gently out of the terminal.

Sue Ellen was enjoying herself. In fact, she was quite carried away with the wine, with the charm and masculinity of her escort, and by the giddiness brought on by the feeling of doing something forbidden. They had been at lunch for over two hours now, and still they lingered, neither one of them wanting to leave. Sue Ellen's eyes were bright with the fever of the moment, and her face was flushed to a lovely shade of pink. Cliff picked up the wine bottle and was about to refill her glass when she put her hand over it, giggling. "Don't you think I've had enough?" she said, with an air of naughtiness.

"Oh, come on now," he said, the devil in his eyes, "this is the glass that'll get you really cheered up!"

Sue Ellen laughed out loud, then covered her mouth in embarrassment, looking around to see if she had drawn anyone's attention. She hadn't. "I think I'm cheerful enough, thank you," she whispered.

Cliff smiled, leaning toward her, and whispered back, "Aren't I wonderful? Look at the magic I perform! A beautiful woman walks into my office, depressed as can be, and voila! In a matter of two hours, I turn her into a vision of ecstasy! Not a bad piece of work, don't you think? Now she's not only beautiful, but laughing, too . . ."

Sue Ellen blushed furiously, smiling in spite of herself. "I'm afraid it's just temporary," she said wistfully. "Things will be back to normal pretty soon."

Cliff sensed his moment with the sureness of a man who has been single and attractive all his life. "What's on your calendar for the rest of the afternoon?" he asked, his meaning as clear as could be.

She looked at him as if she didn't understand, or else couldn't quite believe what she was hearing.

He pressed the point. "We've done such a good job on your mood," he explained, his lips parting, "I think we ought to keep you happy for as long as possible. Wouldn't want to let it get away just yet . . ."

Sue Ellen felt aware of herself and of her mounting interest in and reaction to Cliff's suggestion. She wanted this man, and she knew it. She had tried to deny it ever since she had first laid eyes on him, but now, sitting across the table from him, his interest in her clear, she wanted to lead him out of the restaurant to someplace private, secluded, where she could let down her defenses and respond to her emotions. Yet every alarm bell in her mind went off at once, all the cautionary processes telling her to hold back.

"J.R.'s on his way home from New Orleans right now," she said evasively, "he'll be home any minute . . . I really should be getting back . . ."

She was begging him to overrule her, and he knew it. He was breathing hard with excitement now, the moment so strong with attraction that he felt nothing could stop it. "Maybe his flight's been delayed, hmm?" he suggested. "How about you call home and see?" He felt sure she could give some excuse for being delayed, and just as sure that she would do just that.

Sue Ellen went quickly to the phone, her heart racing with anticipation; she could hardly see the dial in front of her. But by the time she got back to the table, Cliff could see that something had happened. The sexual excitement was still there, but there was something else, too. Was it alarm? Anxiety? Whatever it was, he feared that the moment had passed.

"Miss Ellie's been trying to find me all day long," she said, her brow creased with worry. "She told me to get home right now."

Cliff stood up. "Well, what is it? What's the matter?" he wanted to know.

"I don't know," Sue Ellen shot back. "She refused to say until I got there."

Cliff felt the annoyance rising in him. It wasn't Sue Ellen he was annoyed with, either, but with the Ewing power. On their command, people ran, whether they wanted to or not. Once again, that power had frustrated him. This time in a very exasperating way. "You know, Sue Ellen, just because your mother-in-law gives an order doesn't mean you have to follow it like a dog. You're your own person, you know."

But Sue Ellen was adamant. "You don't know Miss Ellie. When she says now, she means yesterday, not 'as soon as you feel like it.'"

Grabbing her purse and starting for the exit, Sue Ellen turned back to Cliff suddenly realizing how he must be feeling. "We'll have to take a rain check on our afternoon together," she apologized. She disappeared out the door, leaving behind her a man so frustrated he could have exploded.

They had been completely silent all the way home, the enormity of the recent events slowly sinking in on Pam and weighing more and more heavily on both of them. Now, as the car turned off the main road at the entrance to Southfork Ranch and passed under the big iron gate, Pam motioned to Ray to stop the car. He obediently pulled over, knowing that she needed to get herself together for the great deception that was being demanded of her at her weakest moment.

For the last ten minutes, Pam had been trembling throughout the length of her entire body as the bleak prospect of life without Bobby loomed in front of her like an open grave. The pressure of her pent-up emotions rose to an unbearable level. Feeling that the dam was about to burst, she reached for her purse and fumbled inside it for a handkerchief. But with the clutter of the handbag and the trembling of her hands, she was unable to locate it. Finally she gave up, throwing the bag to the floor of the car in fury. The sobs broke from her like a storm on a summer evening. She sat there, powerless, helpless, completely lost and bereft. Tears streamed down her cheeks and dropped on the car seat. Ray silently reached over and, taking her bag, found the handkerchief she'd been looking for and handed it to her.

Finally the river of tears began to run dry, and Pam began to feel the healing effect of a good cry. She wiped her face, and, looking at herself in the rearview mirror, tried as best she could to repair the damage with a little makeup. Turning to him, she nodded, signaling that she was ready.

Ray took her hand and gave it a squeeze of encouragement. "You're gonna be all right now," he said.

She squeezed his hand back, grateful for his sensitivity, glad for his support and company. She would be all right, for the moment, anyway. Taking a deep breath, she faced forward as he put the car back into gear and headed toward the house.

Jock sat up in his bed, his bathrobe loosely wrapped around him, as he took the glass of water and the pills from his wife. He hated the life of an invalid worse than he hated anything, and he couldn't wait for the day he felt strong enough to go back to ranch work. Being housebound was for the birds, and being tended to by women was even worse. As he swallowed the hated pills, he heard the noise of a car approaching and glanced out the window. "Well," he snorted, "at least somebody's finally here! It's about time." He looked intently until the car stopped and its occupants emerged. "Pam," he reported to his wife, who stood across the room, putting things away.

She looked at her watch and smiled, feeling secretly relieved that at least one plane had come in safely. "She's right on time, Jock. No need to get annoyed."

But Jock did not answer her. He was still looking out the window as the other occupant emerged from the driver's seat. "How come Ray's the chauffeur today? Doesn't he have enough to do? If he doesn't, I'll give him something to do, all right. And where's Bobby, anyway? Wasn't he supposed to pick up Pam?"

Ellie fought down the pang that rose up from her stomach at the mention of her son's name. There was still no news, and her worry was rising with each passing minute. But her concern for her husband's health overrode all her other considerations. After all, she thought, one has to tend to the living first. Again she pushed down the horrible thoughts that gnawed at her insides. "Bobby and J.R. aren't back yet," she said off-handedly. "Did you take your pill?"

Jock thrust the empty glass back at her, annoyed. "Why are you always nagging at me, woman?" he shouted. "Why I put up with it is beyond me, it truly is."

Ellie smiled. He was so like a cranky baby sometimes. "You put up with me because you're crazy about me, that's why," she said. "Now you get dressed. I'm going down to get supper ready. You like things on time, I notice, and supper's going to be on time if I have anything to say about it." She turned and marched out of the room.

Jock sighed, disgusted, and began to do as his wife had ordered. Damn it, she was right. He was crazy about her.

Pam entered the house just as Miss Ellie was coming down the stairs. The two women ran to one another and embraced, united in their suffering and grief. After a moment, Ellie stepped back without letting go of Pam, and studied her face. In spite of the quick fix in the car, the ravages of crying were evident. "Go on upstairs and wash yourself off before Jock sees you," she said. Pam wanted to say something, anything, although she didn't know what. But she merely nodded, afraid that if she opened her mouth she would start to cry again. "I'm just going to call in to see what's happening down there," Miss Ellie informed her. And she went off to do so. Pam stared after her for a moment, awed by the strength of the woman who was her mother-in-law, a woman who might have lost two sons, yet whose mind was on the business at hand. Pam felt inspired to do the same. This was no time to give in to fears and grief. There was hope yet, and then, there was Jock. Miss Ellie was right—he had to be kept from the truth until the truth was known. She turned quickly and headed up the stairs to her room.

Miss Ellie was already on the line with Bert. "What's the latest, Bert?" she wanted to know.

"Nothing new, Mrs. Ewing," he replied. "I just talked to search headquarters. Earl's got every spare chopper and plane up in the air, but it's rough up there. The storm's still blowing, and they can't see a thing."

Ellie's face grew tight with pain, aware that with each passing hour, the chances for rescue grew slimmer and slimmer. "All right, Bert. Thank you. I think I'm going to call Earl personally. I want to get the whole picture." And with that, she hung up to make the call.

Pam walked down the hall from her bedroom, past the closed door behind which she could hear Jock singing to himself as he washed his face. So far, so good. She continued on, descending the stairs, and was about to go in to Miss Ellie, when the front door burst open and Sue Ellen entered, flushed and breathless, and a bit unsteady from all the wine at lunch.

"Where's Miss Ellie?" she cried, "I've got to see her!"

Pam shushed her, afraid her cries would draw Jock's attention. She took Sue Ellen's arm and drew her into the living room.

Sue Ellen followed meekly, taken off her guard, but by the time they had entered the big room she had recovered her equilibrium and yanked her arm away. "What is all this about?" she demanded to know. "What in the world is going on here?"

Instead of answering her, Pam went straight over to the bar and poured a drink, filling the glass as far as she could. She brought the drink to her sister-in-law, holding it out for Sue Ellen to take.

Sue Ellen heard the alarm bells going off as she stared at the subdued, grief-stricken Pam. "Are you trying to hide something from me?" she gasped. "What is it? Why was Miss Ellie trying to call me?"

Pam took Sue Ellen's hands and wrapped them around the drink. "Drink this first," she advised. Her voice was firm, and the statement was a command.

Still, instead of taking the glass from her, Sue Ellen's hands dropped to her side. "What is it . . .?" she whispered hoarsely.

"It's Bobby and J.R.," said Pam, her own voice choking as she spoke. "Their plane went down in a storm . . . somewhere in Cado Swamp . . ."

Sue Ellen's face stretched wide in disbelief and horror. "No!" she cried, "It can't be true! It isn't true . . . no!"

Pam took a step toward her, trying to comfort her. "Sue Ellen," she began, but the other woman turned away violently.

"I'm okay," she insisted, "I'll be okay . . . okay . . ." She sat down on the sofa, collapsing in disbelief and shock.

Again Pam offered her the drink. "Take this, Sue Ellen," she said, "I know you need it."

Blindly, in a daze, Sue Ellen took the drink and downed it in one gulp. Pam sat down next to her,

41

waiting a moment for Sue Ellen to recover sufficiently. When she judged her ready to listen, she went on. "Jock doesn't know about it, and Miss Ellie wants it to stay that way."

Sue Ellen nodded, understanding at once, always one to keep the truth from people when it was unpleasant. "When did it happen?" she wanted to know. "How long ago?" She was thinking the unbearable thought that, while she had been with J.R.'s arch enemy, contemplating going to bed with him, her husband had been dying a horrible death. The guilt was overwhelming.

"Just a couple of hours ago. There's already a search underway. They'd been tracking the plane, on Traffic Control Radar, and they have it pinpointed within ten miles in any direction."

She stopped short, hearing footsteps behind her, afraid that it was Jock. But it was Miss Ellie coming in from the study. Her voice was trembling as she said, "They can't find them anywhere. No sign at all . . ."

Sue Ellen sprang up, her whole body protesting against the facts. She banged her glass down on the end table in anger. "But you just said they know where they are! Within ten miles! Surely they must be able to find them within ten miles!"

It was all too much for Miss Ellie. The strain of all those hours, holding everything back, had taken its toll on her. Now something snapped inside her, and the tears came, freely, unblocked, and bitter. "I just spoke to the head of the search team . . . there's not a sign of them . . ."

Pam rushed to embrace the tottering matriarch. "Oh, Miss Ellie . . . keep your hopes up! They may still be all right! You said so yourself, and you were right . . . I can see that myself now! You've got to keep your courage up—for Jock, if for no other reason!"

Miss Ellie nodded, sighing, and pulled herself back together. "That storm is still so bad . . . there really isn't anything they can do till it dies down . . ."

Pam gasped. "What? You don't mean to say they're calling off the search?"

"*NO!*" Sue Ellen shouted. "They can't do that!"

Miss Ellie sighed. "What else *can* they do?" She sobbed woefully, her shoulders shaking uncontrollably in her grief.

Pam embraced her once again. "Please, Miss Ellie, if you break down . . . we'll all . . ." and she too began to cry.

Sue Ellen, unable to contain herself in the face of the open emotions being expressed, began to cry as well, coming to the other two to join in the embrace. The three women were united in fear and grief. Miss Ellie looked up at the ceiling momentarily, and, as if she were addressing God himself, said, "I can't stand it if they're dead . . . Please, don't take both of them . . . not both of them!"

Chapter Three

The crystal chandelier shimmered gaily above the table as the Ewing family, minus its sons, gathered in the dining room for dinner. At the head of the table sat Jock, in his customary place. At the other end sat Miss Ellie, with the bay window behind her, and at her left was the empty chair where Bobby would have been. The chair at Miss Ellie's right was also empty, being J.R.'s traditional place, and the daughters-in-law sat next to the empty chairs, with Lucy on Jock's left. The whole arrangement, fixed as it was in stone, made the table feel particularly empty, even to Jock, who knew nothing of what was going on. If everyone had moved together, closing ranks, the absence of the boys might have been less palpable, less arresting. Their places were set as if they might arrive at any moment. Every part of the charade was seen to with exquisite care, and every last detail was like a knife in the heart of those who knew.

The hardest thing for the women was to keep

their eyes on those present, and off of the empty places. No matter how hard they tried, whenever they thought it was safe to steal a glance, they would find their eyes straying to the empty chairs, and their minds would fill with black thoughts, which they would immediately have to push out of their minds. As difficult as the day had been, this dinner was going to be torture.

For Jock's sake, they kept the conversation going and steered it toward light topics, away from controversy, and especially away from the boys. It wasn't easy. Jock Ewing was a man who liked to argue and to voice his strong opinions on just about everything. Normally the family would hold their own, and the table would be a pretty lively place; but tonight, the women were making every effort to agree with Jock, or at least not to argue with him too much. This last part was not lost on Jock, who thought it definitely peculiar that he was being given his way so easily for a change, but he put it down to the fact that with the boys away, the women were more timid. Jock had lots of opinions about women, more than half of them erroneous.

Miss Ellie took the lead in conversation all through dinner, the girls finding themselves simply unable to move the conversation along on their own. They pushed the food around their plates, occasionally forcing themselves to put a forkful into their mouths and swallow it.

At last dinner was almost over. Ellie had just about run out of dinner conversation, but she did manage to think of one more topic. Turning to Pam, she asked her what New York City had been like. "It's been so many years since I've been there," she said wistfully. Looking at Jock, she reminded him, "It was on our tenth wedding anniversary, Jock, in case you forgot."

Jock smiled and nodded, signifying that he remembered.

Pam put down her fork and knife, grateful not to have to pretend to eat for a few moments, and took up the conversation. It was something easy for her to talk about since it was fresh in her mind and had nothing to do with anything of current importance. "Well," she said, "to be really honest with you, I don't think I spent more than an hour outside of the hotel between showings in the meeting rooms, and meetings in the suite, and meals with Liz in the hotel restaurants . . . I saw a lot of clothes, that's for sure, but hardly anything of the city . . . certainly not enough to render an informed opinion."

Jock shook his head, amused by his own memory of the big city. "Pam, you didn't miss a thing, believe me," he pronounced sagely.

Ellie put down her silverware, delighted to be invited to an argument that was, so she thought, perfectly safe territory. "Jock Ewing!" she gasped. "Either you have a rotten memory, or you just say whatever comes into your head. I remember our trip very well, and I know you had a grand time in New York! Don't try to deny it, because it's true!"

Jock cleared his throat, unable to deny Miss Ellie's charge. He wasn't about to admit he was wrong, however. "All right, I did have a good time," he squirmed, "but it wasn't the city—it was the lovely lady I happened to be with, and nothing else."

Miss Ellie smiled privately. Jock had an amazing ability to be boorish and courtly at the same time. It was an uncanny talent.

But Jock was not finished with the subject of travel. Having been bested once, he was anxious to divert attention from his defeat and take the argument onto new ground. Turning to Pam, he said, wagging his finger at her, "You know, little lady, I think you ought to consider traveling with your husband next time you go. Sounds like you'd have a lot better time than you did with that Liz Craig lady. She sounds like she's all work and no play. Now, Bobby knows how to show a lady a good time!"

There was a stunned, horrified silence at the table as the name of Bobby Ewing coursed through them all like an electric current. The thought that Pam might never travel with Bobby again, let alone even see him again, twisted her insides into a knot that would not let go. At last Pam managed to catch her breath and force a smile. She hoped Jock hadn't noticed her discomfiture, but she could not imagine that he could be so blind as to be oblivious to it. "Don't get the wrong idea, Jock . . . I had a real good time in New York—my work is a lot of fun, you know . . ." Defending her work at the Ewing dinner table was something she did all the time, and by doing it now, she hoped to deflect his attention.

Jock had noticed something wrong, however, and he could tell now that something was being hidden from him. Wondering what it might be, his mind settled quickly on the logical conclusion. "Oh, I get it," he smiled knowingly, "you and Bobby had a fight, didn't you?"

Miss Ellie came to attention suddenly. The argument for argument's sake was suddenly in danger of becoming an argument in earnest. "Jock!" she admonished him. "Whatever may be going on between Bobby and Pam, it's certainly none of our business. People have a right to their privacy, after all . . ."

Jock was indignant. "Well, if it's none of my business, why is everybody acting so damned strange?"

Jock was on the verge of discovering the truth. Something had to be done to divert his attention, and fast. It was Lucy who managed to come to the rescue. "Strange?" she repeated sweetly, in the tone she affected just before she was about to deliver a dig. "Oh, I don't know . . . I don't think we're acting strange at all . . . just being our normal, happy, carefree selves!" It was a brave move on Lucy's part, knowing as she did that her little joke would arouse Jock's anger, but she was willing to bear the brunt of that anger for the sake of the big secret they were all trying to keep.

Jock slammed down his utensils and half rose from his chair. "Now see here, missy," he growled, "don't you get fresh with me! I won't have it! Not in this house, do you understand?"

Sue Ellen, sensing that Lucy could crumble under the force of Jock's anger assumed what would have been her customary role in the discussion. "Lucy," she warned, "mind your manners and listen to your grandfather."

The little diversion had given Pam time to recover herself. Thinking quickly, she realized that a half-truth was better than none at all. Months of living under the same roof with J.R. Ewing had taught her that the more truth there is in a lie, the more believable it becomes. "To tell you the truth,

Bobby and I did quarrel." She hung her head in suitable embarrassment. "Liz and I got so busy on our trip to New York that I wasn't able to meet Bobby in New Orleans as we'd planned. I called to tell him and he got very upset. It seems he'd gone and made all sorts of romantic preparations, but there was nothing I could do about it . . ." Every word sent a shock of pain through her body, as she reminded herself that those harsh words between her and Bobby might be the last contact she would ever have with him. But she had done the trick.

Jock settled himself back into his chair, a satisfied look on his face. "Ha!" he crowed. "I knew you were all hiding something from me! Can't fool Jock Ewing—nosirree!" And he laughed his big, booming laugh.

Ellie could not help smiling, hearing Jock's infectious laughter, but her smile was really one of gratitude. How brave of Pam, to give so much ground. Ellie knew how sensitive an issue Pam and Bobby's privacy was, and how much Pam had stood on it in the past. Confiding it to Jock was an act of great generosity and sacrifice.

But Jock was not finished with the subject. In fact, having been proven right in his suspicions, he was just warming up. No one had ever accused him of being a sensitive human being where other people's feelings were concerned, and no one ever would. Thinking he was sympathizing with Pam in her quarrel with Bobby, he leaned toward her and said, "I don't care how upset Bobby is. That's no reason for him to stay over in New Orleans and leave you stranded at the airport. That kind of behavior is just unforgiveable, and I'm gonna tell him so as soon as he gets the guts to show his face here! Do you know he had a big meeting with Ben Deering this afternoon? He must have been mighty upset with you to miss that!" He shook his head in puzzlement. "Weirdest thing is how he managed to talk J.R. into staying over and missing the meeting. J.R.'s not a man who takes his business lightly."

This last insinuation was more than Pam could bear. Forgetting herself completely for a moment, she said, "Bobby does not take his business lightly any more than J.R. does! And I'm sure that he would never stand someone up on a business meeting just because he had a fight with me!"

She stopped suddenly, realizing what she had said. It was too late, though. The damage was done. Jock turned to his wife, his eyes piercing. "All right, Miss Ellie, if that's not the reason, then where the hell are those boys?"

Miss Ellie struggled to maintain her composure, pinned in a corner by his eyes. "I thought I told you about that storm, Jock," she said.

"Yeah, you told me about it," he said, dismissing it as an excuse, "but you would have thought they'd at least call!"

Now it was Sue Ellen who came to the rescue. "Well, all I can say is that the phone lines must be down! I know my husband would have called me otherwise. He's very responsible that way."

Everyone, including Jock Ewing, was sensitive enough not to answer that remark. J.R. Ewing was anything but responsible to his wife, and nobody wanted to hurt Sue Ellen any more than she was already hurt.

"Damned funny, if you ask me," said Jock. "Even if the phones are down, you'd have thought they'd find some way to get in touch by now."

"Oh, I don't know," said Lucy wryly, "they're probably having too good a time to even think about us."

The danger had passed, for the moment at least. Dinner proceeded to its conclusion, but the conversation never again came so near to the truth. Steering Jock away from the precipice had taken a lot out of all of them, and they excused themselves as soon as they could to retreat into their private hells, to wait, and worry, and grieve alone.

It was night. The house was quiet as Lucy came down the stairs and entered the living room. Quickly and silently, she made her way to the telephone. Her stride bespoke a sense of purpose. She had made up her mind to take action. She dialed the operator and asked to make a person-to-person call to a Las Vegas number. The crumpled paper with the number on it was held in her free hand, which trembled a bit with the anxiety of the moment. "All right, operator," she said, "I'll speak to anyone in charge at the casino." This last was followed by a wait of some seconds while a responsible party was sent for. Finally, a gruff voice came on the line, asking her what she wanted. "This is Lucy Ewing," she explained, "and I'm trying to find Gary Ewing . . . he's my father . . . I think he used to work for you. He was a dealer, or a croupier, or something . . . do you happen to know where he's working now? I thought he might have left a forwarding address, or a telephone number . . . Gary Ewing, yes. Okay, I'll hold on . . ."

Lucy's back was to the entrance. She did not notice Sue Ellen enter, flushed, and obviously having had at least one too many. Hearing Gary Ewing's name mentioned, Sue Ellen sobered up and quickly made her way to Lucy, grabbing the phone out of her hands before she knew what was happening.

"Hey!" cried Lucy, shocked and surprised. But before she could even make a grab for the phone, Sue Ellen had slammed it back down on the cradle. Lucy flailed at her wildly, but Sue Ellen was able to fend her off.

"Can't you at least have the decency to wait until we know for sure that they'd dead?" she hissed.

Lucy stood her ground daunted by Sue Ellen's fury, sure in her heart of the rightness of her actions. "My father should be here," she insisted. "It's his right! He's their brother, you know, no matter how much you wish he wasn't"

"If Jock decides he wants him to be here," Sue Ellen smirked, "I'm sure he'll get in touch with him."

Lucy tightened her face. "He ought to be here, I don't care what anybody thinks!"

"Yes, you'd like that, wouldn't you, young lady?" Sue Ellen taunted her. "You'd like him here, ready to take over, even before his brothers are buried!"

Lucy was stung. She felt as if she'd been slapped hard across the mouth, and she hated her aunt with a passion at that moment. It was not what she had meant at all, and she was bitter toward Sue Ellen for taking it that way. "That wasn't why I wanted him here, hard as that may be for you to imagine with that grubby little mind of yours. You know, there are people in this world who are not as greedy as you are, Sue Ellen!'' she retorted.

"Why you little brat!'' gasped the older woman. She moved to slap Lucy, but the girl was too quick for her and easily dodged the blow.

"Yes, Sue Ellen, that's right,'' she spat, "I'm a little brat—a little brat by the name of *Ewing!* And I was born a *Ewing,* Sue Ellen—not like you!''

Sue Ellen stopped short, caught by surprise by her niece's unexpected insult. Lucy was warming to her theme now, and poured it on mercilessly. Having been hurt, she was now going to give back as good as she had gotten, and better.

"In fact,'' she said, circling Sue Ellen as if she were a lioness circling her prey, "I'd bet dollars to doughnuts that you're real upset tonight that you haven't got a little brat of your own—a *Ewing* brat, just like me! Because I'm sure it's occurred to you that if your precious hubby is dead, and it sure looks like he is, and you're without a child, you're never gonna inherit Southfork! Never! Never!''

Sue Ellen reeled backwards as if she had been shot through the gut. Lucy, having spent her fury, became aware of the effect of her words, and was instantly sorry. She stepped forward, wanting to apologize, but she was too late. Before she could make her move, Sue Ellen had turned, clutching her stomach, and run wildly from the room.

Chapter Four

In the sumptuous luxury of the master suite upstairs, Miss Ellie sat in front of her makeup mirror brushing her hair, her mind miles away, searching Cado Swamp in imagination. Her hand slowly lowered itself, the comb it held forgotten, as she found and embraced her sons. The sensation was so powerful that it might have been real. She sat there for a long time and might have stayed that way even longer until Jock came upstairs from the study, but for the ringing of the phone. It startled her out of her reverie, but it took at least three rings for her to realize where she was and that her mind had been playing tricks on her. A wave of pain rushed over her as she reached for the receiver, half hoping, half dreading, the news from the other side of the line. But it was not Earl, or Bert, or anyone else from the search party. It was Ken Jackson of the *Dallas Press*. From the noise on the other end of the line, she could tell that he was using a phone booth at the airport.

"Mrs. Ewing?" he said, shouting over the noise. "A rumor has just reached my ears that the Ewing family plane has crashed, and that your two sons, Bobby and J.R., were aboard that plane and are missing. Would you care to substantiate or deny the rumor, Mrs. Ewing?"

Miss Ellie's mouth tightened in anger. She had dreaded this moment all day long, and had prayed that somehow the story would not be uncovered, at least until they were certain one way or the other. "I have no comment whatsoever," she replied icily into the phone.

But Jackson was not to be easily deterred. "Well, will you at least confirm or deny that the plane is down? Mrs. Ewing? May I speak with one of your sons, then?"

Fire burned in Miss Ellie's eyes, the fire of sheer outrage. But, as always, she kept her voice under control. "I believe I just heard myself say that there would be no comment. Perhaps you should have your ears checked, Mr. Jackson, or whatever your name is." She hung up the phone quickly before she lost control and said something she would regret later. Immediately she pressed a button on the intercom connecting her with the employees' quarters.

"Yes, ma'am?" she heard Ray's voice on the other end of the line.

"Ray, I'm a little upset," she found herself saying. "I just got off the phone with a reporter. I refused to talk to him, of course, but he won't be the last, I'm sure. There'll be more of them, lots more, and some of them won't be content just to use the telephone. They'll be pouring through the gates in an hour or so, trying to get into the house. I don't want that happening. Get all the ranch hands together and have them close off all the entrances and all the roads on the property. I want a weather eye kept out for all trespassers, understood?"

There was a slight pause, and then Ray asked, "What do you want them to do when they find somebody?"

"I want them taken off the property. Escorted to the gates."

"Will do, Miss Ellie," said Ray, and she hung up, feeling only a little bit more at ease.

Putting her hair back in order, she headed down the stairs to the den, to see how her husband was doing. As she opened the door, she stopped short. There he was, a big cigar in his hand, the cutter in the other. His cigar was lit, and his lips were pursed in the act of blowing out the first delightful rings of smoke. He looked up at her sheepishly, knowing he had been caught red-handed in the act of forbidden pleasure.

She eyed him skeptically, wondering how many times in the past few weeks he had cheated on his regimen in just the same manner. He shrugged, as if to say it couldn't be helped, that, after all, he was merely a fallible, weak man, subject to the temptations that lure everyone, healthy and sick alike. His expression was rueful, contrite, but she knew it was because he had been caught and had caused her pain and worry, and not because he was smoking.

She did not, as she might normally have done, take it from him, knowing as she did that it might be the last pleasure he had for some time, perhaps ever. Instead, she asked him, as if it had not been an object of friction between them, "Is it a good cigar, Jock?"

He nodded, playing along with the charade. "Sure is," he said. "I have you to thank for keeping the humidor full." It was a subtle way of shifting the blame onto her, but it was only in jest.

"Old habits die hard," she acknowledged. "Especially bad ones." She gave him a meaningful look.

"It would be even better with a little brandy."

She took the cigar out of his hand. "I know. Too bad you won't be having any—or any more of this, either." She put it out in the ashtray.

He looked at it sadly, the symbol of all the lost pleasures of his past. "I married a hard woman," he shook his head.

"You married a woman with discipline, and thank God somebody around here has some. You sure don't. And even if it kills you, you're going to follow the doctor's instructions as long as I'm here to enforce them."

"Even if it kills me, huh?" He smiled. "So that's what we're trying to do, is it? I thought we were trying to avoid my demise at all costs."

Suddenly Ellie was caught up short, not sure for a moment whether he knew the truth and was letting her know it in a roundabout, subtle way. She glanced at him, trying to read his thoughts. He was watching her, his face a blank, giving away nothing, no hint of what was behind those hawk's eyes of his. She stared at him for as long as she dared, then, deciding she'd better keep up the front, smiled cheerfully again.

"Sorry," she said, "I guess I could have found a better way of putting it at that." She leaned over and kissed him tenderly on the forehead. "But you're still recovering, Jock. Heart bypass surgery is no laughing matter. And I'm not about to let you throw your life away just because you can't control your appetites. I need you, you know." She sighed, her reasons a secret. "More than I can say."

Away from the big house, as far away as she had the strength to go, Pam walked aimlessly, senselessly, her compressed emotions sending her in varied directions, the light of the full moon the only protection she had against stumbling over a tree root or blundering into some nocturnal animal. Out where she was, the stillness and silence of the Texas night were overwhelming, and the stars shone down in their billions, their light diminished only by the stronger nearer light of the moon. Looking up at it for long periods at a time, Pam's mind wandered through the memories of her relationship with Bobby . . . their meetings at those Ewing barbeques when she had been, of all things, Ray Krebbs' girlfriend, but Ray had been too drunk to pay any attention to her . . . the first time Bobby brought her back to Southfork, and J.R. immediately tried to buy her off the ranch and out of the Ewing family . . . the pregnancy and the fight that had resulted in her miscarriage . . . the crazy chase after Lucy when she had run away and fallen into a criminal's clutches . . . the tender and wild moments in bed, when she had explored a realm of closeness and ecstasy she had never known before, whose existence she had been totally unaware of, and would have remained ignorant of if it had not been for Bobby . . . her Bobby . . . her love. She wondered if the same bright moon she was looking at shone down on him; if he was hurt, or lost . . . perhaps he was dying at that very moment, or just coming awake from a long period of unconsciousness. The agony of her thoughts was tearing her heart apart, and she had to force herself to tow the line—Bobby was alive. He had to be. At least, until they knew otherwise, she could not allow the dreadful speculations to enter her mind . . . but how? Oh, how could she stop them? Exhausted by the hurricane inside her, she sank down against a fencepost and wept bitter tears, shivering with the fear of a life alone, without Bobby, without her dearest, dearest love.

In the tack room of the Southfork stables, Ray gathered the ranch hands together to explain their orders to them. He did not tell them why they were to do what they were to do, only that the orders were issued by Miss Ellie and that Jock was to remain unaware of their activities.

"There will be two of you men on every road leading to the ranch, sealing off all access, and besides that, I want a man at every gate, standing guard with a rifle. Sawhorses across the roads, too. Is that clear?"

There was a lot of coughing and shuffling around in discomfort, but no one raised any objections. Knowing their employers as they did, they knew there must be a good reason for the bizarre orders, and an equally good reason why they weren't being let in on it.

"We have six or seven four-wheel drive vehicles. I want them riding the fences all up and down the ranch. I don't want any reporters getting through to Ewing land. Not until Miss Ellie says it's okay."

One of the hands shook his head. "Hey, Ray,

that's a lot of ground to cover with just six trucks," he protested.

"Yes, well, it's all fenced, right?" Ray rejoined. "That makes a trespasser out of anybody who's found on this side of the fence."

The ranch hands looked at each other warily. From the back of the room somebody let out a low whistle. "We going to shoot somebody if we find 'em, Ray?" someone asked.

"No," said Ray softly, "no violence. If you get hold of somebody who's got no business being on the ranch, just escort 'em off it again, and quickly. Don't bruise 'em, just keep 'em far away from the big house, and get 'em out of here as fast as possible. Understood?"

The men nodded, relieved that they would not have to shoot at anyone. One by one, they silently filed out to begin fulfilling their mysterious commission.

The fire blazed red and blue sending waves of warmth across the room to the desk where Jock sat poring over his ledgers, keeping an eye on the family's investment portfolio, entering notes and figures, silently gathering thoughts on what purchases and sales might be called for in the coming week. Seated across from him, Miss Ellie held open a book, pretending to read, now and again stealing a glance at her husband just to make sure he was still there, that he still didn't know what was going on all around him. She had to give herself credit for getting this far without giving anything away. It had been a monumental achievement, and it had cost her plenty in terms of emotional expenditure. She prayed that before too long she would have some news, even if it was bad news. Nothing could be worse than this uncertainty, this pretense. On the outside, she had managed to maintain her placid, everyday appearance and demeanor, but on the inside, a hurricane raged unchecked, tossing her heart to and fro. She was not a young woman anymore, and she did not know how long she could bear it. Yet she knew she must bear it, that she had to keep her husband alive at all costs. The shock of the crash had been so hard on her, she could only imagine what effect it would have on a man recovering from open heart surgery.

Finally Jock closed the book, his calculations done for the time being, and turned to his wife, a satisfied smile on his face. "Miss Ellie," he said, "it's been a long time since we got to spend time together like this, just the two of us. Too long, that's for sure."

Miss Ellie nodded slowly. Just the two of them indeed. Soon, they might be just the two of them for always. The thought was almost too much to bear, not because she didn't enjoy spending time with Jock, but because her life would be over if her boys were indeed dead. "I don't think we've had that kind of time together since before the boys were born," she replied, each syllable causing her unutterable pain. "Having children sure makes for a busy life, doesn't it, Jock?"

Her husband had been studying her face. She was still a good looking woman. She certainly had aged well, he reflected with a certain amount of egotistical pride. "Miss Ellie, you know you look as young as you did then. I swear it."

She laughed heartily, genuinely amused even in

the midst of her agony. "You're a liar, Jock Ewing. I'm a lot older, and a lot fatter, and a lot grayer, and you know it!" She wiped the tears from her eyes and stopped laughing with a sigh.

He went to her and knelt down before her. "Not in my eyes, you aren't." he whispered tenderly. "And even that quack doctor knows there isn't anything wrong with my vision, wreck of a man that I am." Looking deeply into each other's eyes, they kissed, holding each other's heads in their hands, in close touch for one moment with all that was inside of them. She held him tightly for a while, hiding her face from him so that he could not see the fear and pain lighting her face like a beacon of distress. At last she was able to pull herself together, and let go of him. When he saw her face again, it was painted with a bright smile of affection.

"Well, young man, I think it's time for all you kids to go to bed," she joked, imitating the voice of a kiddie show host from the old days.

"Now, Miss Ellie," he complained, "how can a man sleep if he's feeling wide awake? It's plumb impossible! You know that as well as I do! Besides, you and that quack doctor don't let me get any activity at all during the day—all I do is sit around! How's a man supposed to get tired like that?"

"Never you mind," his wife insisted. "Just go on up to the bedroom. Read if you don't feel like sleeping. Relax a little."

"Relax, hell!" he boomed back at her in protest, "I hate books, you know that!" And, without waiting for her to respond, he reached over to turn on the television set. Alarmed, Miss Ellie frantically searched inside herself for a way to

63

distract him from his purpose. She couldn't chance him hearing a news flash, and yet she didn't want to arouse his suspicion.

Suddenly it came to her. "All right, Jock Ewing, if you don't want to sleep, we might as well play some backgammon." She knew she had him with that one. He hadn't won a game from her in months, although he kept on insisting it was just dumb luck, and he was always ready for a grudge match. "If you insist on staying awake, I insist on having you all to myself. I'm not going to let some pretty anchorwoman cast a spell over you."

"What stakes?" he asked warily. She was always insisting they play for pennies so that he wouldn't lose too much and get angry. "Pennies again, I suppose."

She grinned at him with a gleam in her eye. "What the heck?" she whispered conspiratorially. "Let's go for a nickel!" And with that, they set to it and played all through the eleven o'clock news.

Sue Ellen stood alone at the bar in the corner of the living room pouring herself another drink. Her hands were unsteady and her body swayed from side to side, but it was only partially from the liquor. She drank a lot these days, and her body was learning how to function under the influence of greater and greater amounts of alcohol. But the stress of the moment, combined with her inability to eat much of anything at supper, had just about done her in.

One more drink, she told herself, and then no more. For a while. No more for a while, absolutely not, girl. You've had enough. Imagine you being so shook up over J.R.'s probable demise when he's been the cause of so much grief for you almost since the day he married you! Why, you wouldn't be drinking today if it weren't for him!

Thus went Sue Ellen's thoughts as she held the clear glass of vodka up to the light. Suddenly, looking up at the chandelier made her woozy, and she reached out a hand to steady herself against the bar. She noticed with satisfaction that she hadn't spilled any of her drink and quickly took another sip in order to prevent spillage. It was only after she had done so, and turned to head for the privacy of her bedroom, that she noticed Pamela standing in the doorway looking at her with an odd expression on her face. It wasn't disapproval, exactly . . . yet it wasn't sympathy either. Looking right back at her combatively, out of habit really, Sue Ellen raised the glass in a toast and downed it in one gulp.

"I think you've had enough to drink, Sue Ellen," said Pam, who had just returned from her solitary walk and was heading for the bar herself.

"How much is enough?" Sue Ellen shot back coyly. "Enough all depends on whom you're talking about. In my case, enough means whatever it takes to put me to sleep." She nodded, her eyes satisfied slits turned inward to consider the wisdom of her last remark. "Yes, that would be just about enough, I think."

Pam felt suddenly touched by this woman who had been nothing but cruel to her ever since she had come to Southfork, and who had always treated her as an enemy, a rival, a usurper of her favored position in the Ewing family. Pam had never liked her; yet now, seeing her vulnerable for the first time, Pam was aware of how difficult a life Sue Ellen must have had married to J.R., a man who treated her like his slave and cheated on her regularly. Her life could not have been very satisfying, in spite of all the wealth and prestige. Pam went to her and put her arm on Sue Ellen's shoulder tenderly. "Let me help you up to your room," she said softly.

But Sue Ellen did not want to be led upstairs. Somehow Pam's tender gesture had reached her, pierced her armor, and now she wanted to talk, to pour her heart out to this woman whom she had always regarded as her enemy. "I love my husband!" she wailed in plaintive protest. "Nobody understands that! I really do love him! I tried everything I could think of to make him love me . . ." She trailed off, her voice choked with unshed tears.

Pam felt the embarrassment of unsought confidences, and she tried to stave of any further soul-baring, feeling it would only make the wall between them higher in the end. "Don't, Sue Ellen," she counseled. "That kind of talk will only make things harder on you."

But Sue Ellen, lost in maudlin contemplation of her tragic fate, ignored Pam's words and continued to pour out her secret heart. "I've been in here for over an hour just making a list in my head . . . a list of all the blessings I've been granted in my life . . . and guess what? I owe them all to J.R. . . . every last one of them. My country club membership . . . my status in the community . . . all the parties I give and get invited to . . . everything has come to me because my husband is J.R. Ewing. That's the only reason I am what I am."

Everything in Pam's nature rebelled against the spectacle of this woman denigrating her own worth, debasing her own attributes. "No, Sue Ellen, no!" she cried in protest. "None of what you say is true. Look at yourself—why, you're beautiful . . . you're intelligent . . . There are lots of other things you could be doing with yourself."

Sue Ellen only half heard her, the alcoholic fog filtering Pam's words and selecting which ones would get through and which fell on deaf ears. "You know," she said, smiling, "today I had lunch with a very attractive man. And he thought I was beautiful, too . . ." A sad thought occurred to her, spoiling her happy memory of Cliff. "Of course, he's probably only attracted to me because I'm Mrs. J.R. Ewing. It's all because of that. Everything comes down to that . . ."

Pam took the empty glass out of Sue Ellen's hands. "This," she said, holding up the glass before Sue Ellen's eyes, "is also because you're Mrs. J.R. Ewing." Sue Ellen frowned, yanking her hand out of Pam's grasp. "Come on, Sue Ellen," Pam pressed on, leaving her previous remark to sink in as it might, "I'll help you get up to your room."

Something had clicked in Sue Ellen, however, and just as Pam had feared, the wall between them was once again thrown up, higher and nastier than ever. "I see how you're looking at me," she smirked. "Poor Sue Ellen, isn't that it? You pity me, don't you? Ha! That's a laugh! Let's see how you feel about being just plain Pamela Barnes again."

Pam gasped, stung by the certainty of death implied by Sue Ellen's remark. "Don't say things like that!" she insisted. "They're all right! Both of them! They have to be! They have to come back!"

Sue Ellen saw that she had hit a nerve, and she smiled with satisfaction that she had made someone more miserable than she. "Not a very pleasant prospect, is it, Pamela?" she drawled cheerfully. She began circling her sister-in-law slowly, regarding her from all angles as she did so, seeming to see through her, the alcohol sending glimmers of her own deep suspicions to the light of her eyes. "You're so good at pretending, aren't you, Pamela?" she said, tauntingly. An edge of hardness sounded in her voice, hinting of the fierce hatred she harbored, unexpressed until now. "I've always known you were just a gold-digger . . . a money-hungry gold-digger, that's what you've always been."

Pam was flabbergasted. Even allowing for Sue Ellen's drunken condition, and for the hostility, she never thought Sue Ellen's hatred of her went so very deep. Her own anger welled up inside her, and she snapped back, "That's all you can think about, isn't it, Sue Ellen? All the things you can buy with Ewing money?"

But Sue Ellen was once again lost in maudlin contemplation. She gazed around the room, at every precious object and furnishing, as if it were the last time she would ever see them. "Goodbye forever . . ." she muttered, lost in the fog of her personal loss.

"Oh, come off it, Sue Ellen," Pam said sternly, out of patience. "I'm not going to listen to you sloshing around in your own self-pitying tears, counting up all your losses to yourself just like a miser about to go broke."

Sue Ellen's gray haze gave way to red fury. "Don't you dare speak to me like that!" she screamed. "Your husband yanked you up right out of the gutter. How many men paid your way in life until you found a nice rich Ewing boy to pick up the check for you?''

Crack! The sound of Pam's hand slapping Sue Ellen's face resounded in the big empty room, echoing for several seconds in the stunned silence that followed. Sue Ellen ran to pour herself another drink, but her hands were so unsteady that she spilled half of it.

"For your information," raged Pam, "I have paid my own way all my life! No man ever took care of my bills—I've worked at jobs since I was a kid—I still do work at a job! Have you ever in your life held down a job, Sue Ellen? Have you? Answer me!"

But Sue Ellen could not answer. Her meager defenses had crumbled from the force of Pam's counterattack, and she lapsed once again into self-pity. "If J.R. is dead, it's the end of me . . . I'll lose everything . . . everything . . ." She looked at Pam piteously. "I don't even have a baby. And I wanted one more than anything . . ." she sobbed.

Pam, too, broke into tears, the memory of her own child reflected for her in the grief of the wrecked woman before her. The two women reached out for each other, instinctively taking each other in their arms, blotting out for the moment whatever was between them, their grief and their loss the only realities in their shattered worlds.

Chapter Five

Ellie came down the stairs breathing a long sigh of relief now that her day of dissembling was finally over. No more hiding things till morning at least. As she reached the foyer, the front door opened and Ray let himself into the house.

"I didn't want to announce myself," he said, explaining why he hadn't rung the doorbell as he usually would have done.

Miss Ellie understood perfectly well. "I just now managed to get Jock to bed," she said.

"Any news yet?" he asked, already knowing the answer. If there had been news, he would have been able to tell by her expression.

Miss Ellie shook her head. "I spoke to Earl about twenty minutes ago. The storm is finally over, and they're starting to send out more planes." She scrutinized him for a moment. "How's it going out there?" she inquired.

Ray smiled, satisfied. "We had to turn back a bunch of reporters and cameramen at the front gate. They asked some questions, but the hands didn't tell them anything . . . they didn't know anything, so there was nothing to tell." Ellie shot him a grateful smile.

Suddenly there was a light tapping at the front door. The two of them looked at each other apprehensively, wondering who could be knocking at the door at such a late hour.

Miss Ellie went to answer it, and when the door opened, she saw a slight, rather nervous-looking young man standing there, a look of uneasy determination on his face. "What do you want?" said Miss Ellie unceremoniously.

"Uh, my name is . . . uh . . . Ken Jackson . . . from the *Press*—I called earlier today."

"You happen to be trespassing on private property, mister," Ray advanced toward him threateningly.

But Miss Ellie waved him back. "That's all right, Ray," she said, wearily, "I'll take care of this fellow myself." Stepping forward, she backed the intruder out onto the veranda until they were both outside the house. "How did you manage to get in, Mr. Jackson?" she asked, a harsh edge to her voice. When he hesitated, she repeated, "How did you get in, I said?"

The reporter was on the defensive, unsure of his ground, yet still determined to get his story. "Um . . . I don't know if you remember, Mrs. Ewing," he stammered, "but a couple of years back, I did a story on Southfork for the paper. I happened to remember a ravine that ran through into your feed lot."

Miss Ellie nodded, annoyed. "We'll have to plug up that hole," she muttered. "Now, then," she continued, staring the little man down. "Now that you've barged your way in here, what is it you want from us?"

Her voice was uncharacteristically cold and hard, so much so that it actually intimidated the reporter, who had had years of experience, and was usually brazen and unflappable. He knew he was invading someone's privacy, and he knew that if the story was true, he was intruding on a family's secret grief. But to him, the right of the people to know was sacred, and, in spite of how intimidated he might personally feel, he did not intend to let that interfere with his getting the facts of the story and printing them.

"Well, uh . . . I guess what I wanted . . . if you could possibly give me a statement? Just something simple, to satisfy my editor." Ken Jackson knew how to worm information out of people. It was going to be difficult this time, but he would do it somehow.

"When I spoke to you on the phone," Miss Ellie said evenly, "I gave you a few words. They were, I believe, to the effect that I had no comment."

Jackson shuffled his feet in discomfort. "Well," he explained, "I thought that, as time went on, you might have more to say. Now that you've had time to reflect . . ."

Miss Ellie was about to lose her temper. Ever since she had married Jock Ewing, her life had been an open book to the press, and the doings of her family had been widely reported both in newspapers and on television. She had always found it distasteful to be so exposed, as if she were fair game for strangers, but she had always been gracious about it, understanding that it came along with being rich and powerful. But this, now, at such a traumatic moment, was not to be borne.

"Mr. Jackson," she said, her voice rising in spite of herself, "you come into possession of a rumor, a rumor that an airplane has crashed, that my two sons are missing, and immediately, without a second thought, without a consideration for our family's feelings, our privacy, or our grief, you come skulking around like a jackal in search of carrion! Someone has to teach you a lesson, so that you learn once and for all to respect the privacy of individuals. Ray," she said, reaching out a hand behind her, but not taking her eyes off the now terrified reporter, "get the hunting rifle out of the storage closet, will you?"

"Sure will, ma'am," said a grinning Ray, happy to see the reporter in such obvious discomfort.

The poor little man stared at the Ewing matriarch, uncertain, having a hard time believing this gentle, mild-mannered woman might actually be serious, might actually take a hunting rifle to him, but not quite sure she wouldn't, either. He felt he had better say something, fast, to allay her anger. "Look, Mrs. Ewing," he said, chuckling nervously, "I'm a reporter. This is my job, whether I like it or not."

Miss Ellie held her ground, however, her rage unabated. "You'd better look for a better job, Mr. Jackson. Or find another way to do the one you have."

Ray returned with the shotgun, still grinning at the comical prospect of Miss Ellie scaring someone off with a rifle. Ellie took the gun in her hands as if she'd been a marksman all her life. In fact, she'd taken target practice not a few times, and was a fair shot. She pointed the rifle at Jackson's forehead, no emotion showing, seeming for all the world as if she were prepared to shed his blood with no regrets. The reporter backed off a step, scared now to within an inch of his life, sorry that his ingenuity had brought him this close to danger.

"You, sir," said the riflewoman, "are on Southfork property without express permission and, therefore, are a trespasser. My daddy would have blown you to bits by now, and I won't even begin to describe what my husband would have done to you. So, unless you hightail it out of here in less than five seconds, I'm going to fill you so full of buckshot that you'll never get it out. Now get out of here—pronto! Understood?"

Jackson was retreating, falling all over himself in his hurry to get out without taking his eyes off the rifle that was pointed at him. "Okay . . . okay . . . just don't shoot! I'm going . . ." He turned and started to run, hoping to get out of range before he heard the dreadful report behind him.

On the veranda, Ray chuckled softly in satisfied admiration. Miss Ellie had shown him a side of herself he had never seen before, and never even knew existed. "I'll get a couple of the boys on that ravine," he said, turning to leave. "Never know who else might get a bright idea." Tipping his hat to her in tribute, he stepped off the porch into the moonlit night.

With Ray and the reporter gone, Ellie felt the strength she had mustered drain right out of her like air out of a punctured balloon. She felt suddenly faint, trembling from head to foot. She leaned against the doorpost for support, the world spinning around her. All the agony, the anxiety, and the strain of the day came rushing in on her at once, and for a moment she really did think she would black out right there on the porch. She gathered herself, however, and after a moment was able to let go of the doorjamb and turn to go inside. That was when she saw him.

Jock stood on the stair landing, fully dressed, his face black with rage and despair. He stared at her as if he had never known her till this moment. "*Why*, Ellie?" he said, his voice a low growl of pain.

Ellie knew at once that the game was over. "You heard everything we said," she said, her world falling apart.

He nodded gravely and descended the stairs toward her. "Why did you keep it from me?" He grabbed her arm, pulling her close to him, her head bending back to stare into his eyes, eyes that were aflame.

"Oh, Jock," she whispered, "I was so afraid you'd have an attack! That you might die on me! If I'd lost my boys, I didn't want to lose you, too! Don't you see?" She began to cry, all the tears she had held back all day coming freely now, now that there was no reason to hold them back.

Jock released her arm, roughly pushing her away from him, not so much in anger as in despair. "Goddammit, woman!" he roared. "I'm all right! When are you going to see that?" He turned his back to her, hiding the tears that were coming to his eyes, too. He would not let her see them, not give her that. From the shelter of his position, he whispered hoarsely, "Both of them . . . damn . . . damn!"

"We don't know for sure yet, Jock," Miss Ellie hastened to tell him. "There's a full search going on for them now that the storm's over. There's still hope . . . we mustn't give up on them yet . . ."

Jock turned back to her, scanning her eyes to make sure she was telling him the truth. Satisfied that she was, he nodded gravely and headed for the door, striding firmly like a man with a mission.

"Wait, Jock!" she called after him. "What are you going to do?"

"What do you think I'm going to do?" he shot back at her. "I'm going to join the search party, that's what I'm going to do."

She ran to him, grabbing onto his arm for dear life, sure that if he went, she would never see him again, aware as she was of his fragile health. However much he might insist that he was all right, the doctor had insisted on lots of rest for at least another month or so.

"I won't let you go, Jock!" she cried, "You can't take it! It will be too much for you, I know it! Please stay, Jock! Please! For me, if for no other reason!"

He stood there unmoved. She looked up at him, showing him with her eyes how much she loved him, needed him, and feared for him. At last he understood why she had kept it from him, and he was moved, moved that he could still inspire such fierce love in so grand and good a woman.

"Please, Jock . . . I beg you . . ."

Finally he relaxed, nodding assent. "Okay, Ellie," he muttered. "I'll have Ray go instead."

Relieved, Miss Ellie collapsed against her husband and wept her first free tears.

Ray sat opposite his boss staring at him across the great oak desk. He owed everything to Jock Ewing, and he loved him like a father, the father he had never had. He would have done anything for this man, and it pained him to see the grief that was ravaging the old man's face. Jock, too, was equally pained. The awareness of his dependence on the younger, stronger man was almost unbearable to him, accustomed as he was to handling everything himself, to being limitlessly strong and capable. Incapacity was an anathema to him, but now he was having to learn to live with it. Painstakingly, making sure Ray heard and understood every last instruction to the letter, he went over the points one by one, over and over again. It was after two in the morning now, and in a couple of hours the planes would be up again searching for the boys. There was time now for preparation before it was light, and Jock needed to make sure Ray was prepared, prepared as he himself would have been. It might make all the difference.

"Earl McCrady's already been told you'll be coming along on the search," Jock was saying. "They'll be going up again at daybreak, so you'll need to get to the airfield about an hour before then . . . that'll be about, say, three-thirty."

Ray nodded, taking everything in, just the way he knew Jock wanted him to.

"From what I understand, having talked to Earl," Jock continued, "the homing beacon on their plane isn't working. That means one of three things. Either it's busted, or it got lost in the crash, or Johnnie's too badly hurt to set it up and turn it on. So, I want you to be looking for something else, a different kind of signal." Jock had shut out all emotion for the time being, his every fiber taut, braced, and in position for the job at hand. "When J.R. was a boy," he went on, "we used to spend a lot of time together. We'd go out hunting, fishing, camping. He was just a kid at the time, but he wanted to go along with me wherever I went. So I taught him a system of signals for whenever he was lost or hurt, or out alone when night fell. I drilled it into him, and I know he'll remember it—if he's alive. The code is three of anything, Ray—three flares, three fires, three flashes, three of anything. I want you to look for that, all right?"

"Yes sir." Ray nodded. "I'll be looking for it. Three of anything. Any other instructions?"

Jock was silent for a moment, deep in his own thoughts. When he looked back at Ray, there was deep pain in his eyes. "Yes, Ray . . . there is something else. No matter what happens . . . whether they're dead or alive . . . I want my boys back home. Bring them back home to me Ray."

Ray fought back his own emotions. His voice a whisper, he replied, "I will, sir. I promise."

Miss Ellie tiptoed across the upstairs hallway and knocked softly on the door of Sue Ellen's bedroom. There was no answer, and Miss Ellie, after a moment of hesitation, opened the door a crack and looked inside. Sue Ellen was lying across the bed, fully clothed and fast asleep, the vast amount of alcohol having finally brought her the peace she sought. Her mouth was open and she was snoring softly. Across the room the window was wide open, and the chilly wind blew the curtains up in white billowing clouds. Entering silently and taking a quilt from the chest, Ellie covered her daughter-in-law and shut the window most of the way. She looked sadly down at the sleeping face beneath her, and her heart went out to the poor woman whose life with J.R. had obviously fallen on hard times, and who now was likely going to be a widow. Heaving a deep sigh, she left the room, quietly pulling the door shut behind her.

Feeling the need to talk to someone, Miss Ellie continued along the corridor, coming at last to Pam's room. The door was slightly ajar, and, peering through, Miss Ellie could see that while Pam, too, was lying across the bed fully clothed, she was wide awake, staring absently at the bedside lamp.

Pam raised her head at the sight of Miss Ellie, her eyebrows arched in worry. "Have you heard anything?" she asked.

Miss Ellie shook her head, and, coming into the room, shut the door behind her. "Jock knows," she said.

Pam gasped in surprise. "He's okay?" she wanted to know.

"Well, I think he is. He's sending Ray out with instructions to join the search."

Pam nodded, understanding this as confirmation that Jock was, indeed, all right. If he was giving orders, he couldn't be in such bad shape. She pushed some photographs out of the way so that Miss Ellie could sit next to her on the bed, and reached for one. It was a photo of Pam and Bobby in New Orleans. "Those are some shots we took when we were on our honeymoon last year," she explained, needlessly. "There were just a few . . . we should have taken more." She looked up at Ellie, stricken with grief and pain.

Ellie reached for her hand and held it, squeezing it hard. "Oh, Pam," she whispered, "I'm frightened, too. Just as frightened as you are. I don't think I've ever been this scared before in all my life. Not even when Jock went off to war and I didn't hear from him for weeks." She paused, wondering for a moment why, indeed, she hadn't been as scared then as now. "Probably it was because we were both so very young in those days . . . you know, that wonderful age when you think there's no way you can die—'It can't happen to me' and all . . ."

Pam watched her, the reality of Bobby's death settling on her for just a brief moment. Then, with a shiver, she shook it off.

"But now . . ." Ellie continued, about to say again how frightened she was.

Pam stopped her. She had to in order to keep her own demons at bay. "Please, Miss Ellie," she begged, "we mustn't even think about it . . . not yet . . ."

Miss Ellie's thoughts took a different track, still far away, but not as morbid now, Pam's words apparently having sunk in without destroying her reverie. "Those sons of mine . . ." she recalled. "When they were babies, oh, they were something. You should have seen them. You wouldn't believe how shy J.R. was! Whenever I took him shopping, he was always grabbing hold of my skirt, following me wherever I went. At first, Jock scared him with his loud voice and his rough ways. But then, when I had Gary, Jock just took over J.R. and practically raised him himself. Jock says he turned him into a man's man. So I guess then I did too much fussing over Gary. Then I had Bobby! And did we ever spoil him! All of us, including J.R. and Gary. J.R. had to fight for everything he ever got, and Gary just didn't bother to try to get anything. But Bobby—he got anything he ever wanted." She sniffed back tears as she came back to the horrible present. "I have always loved them, no matter what they did. I do love them . . . in spite of everything that's happened. I love them all so much . . ." She dissolved in tears, unable to speak another word.

Looking at Pam, she saw the devastating effect her words had had. Pam was close to breaking down completely. Ellie caught herself, choking back a sob, holding herself together for her daughter-in-law's sake. "Oh, don't even listen to me . . . I'm just a rambling old lady, Pam. I came in here to talk, make you feel a little better, and look what a mess I've made of it."

Pam, too, got hold of herself. "Oh, no, Miss Ellie, you mustn't say that. I'm glad you came. And don't worry about me . . . I'll be okay . . . really I will." Ellie nodded, and rising, brushed the wrinkles out of her skirt as she headed for the door.

"Don't give up hope, Pam. I'm not going to. And try to sleep a little. There won't be any news till tomorrow anyway."

After Ellie had gone, Pam turned out the bedside light and lay back on the pillow. But she didn't sleep. Wide awake, filled with dread, memories, and dark imaginings, she stared at the patterns the moon made on the ceiling, and passed a long, wakeful night alone.

Chapter Six

The sun came up on Southfork Ranch, and the new day began. The birds chirped as they did every morning, and the cattle lowed in the barns. It was a day like any other, and yet so very different. The whole world had changed for the Ewing family.

Out on the veranda, Lucy put the finishing touches on the table settings. She had cooked breakfast for herself and Jock, meaning to keep him busy and out of Ellie's way while she dealt with the ongoing search and the pursuit of aggressive reporters. While Pam had already been cued by Miss Ellie, Miss Ellie hadn't had a chance to speak with Lucy yet. And so, when Jock came outside, Lucy was ready for him. "Hey, grandpa, come on over," she chortled.

"How come you got so ambitious today, Lucy?" he asked. "You're usually about as fond of cooking as you are of the plague!"

Lucy shrugged coquettishly. "Why don't you try

it before you make fun of it?" she teased. "I happen to be a great cook. It's one of the world's best kept secrets."

As Jock sat down, he looked straight into his granddaughter's eyes and said, quietly, "By the way, I know everything."

Lucy got the message. Her good humor evaporated the way a puddle does in the desert. "I'm so sorry for all this, Grandpa," she whispered, her eyes brimming over.

Unable to say anything, Jock merely nodded an acknowledgement and forced himself to eat the eggs, which good as they might have been, tasted like ashes to him. Lucy was unable even to eat, and merely pushed her food around with her fork. There was something on her mind, something that had been gnawing at her ever since the crisis had begun.

"Grandpa," she began, timidly, "don't you think my father should be here?"

Jock looked up sternly. His eyes searched hers, looking behind them to get a glimpse of the machinery working in his devious granddaughter's mind. "You've already called him, haven't you?" he asked her.

Lucy hesitated just a bit too long before she answered, "Why, of course not, Grandpa. I'd never do that! You know I wouldn't!"

Rather than berating her for going behind his back, he answered her original question. "Your father had his chance already, Lucy. He left us of his own free will—more than once. He made his own bed, and he's got to lie in it."

"He's still your son!" she cried, bitterness shrill in her throat.

Jock grimaced, her words a knife turning in an open wound. "Be quiet and eat, Lucy," he commanded.

"J.R. and Bobby are his brothers!" she shouted, undaunted.

"I'm not going to talk anymore about it!" Jock bellowed.

They were both standing now, facing each other like pit bulls in the ring. For a moment, there was a stalemate, then, overmatched, Lucy threw down her napkin and ran back into the house. Looking after her, Jock felt for the first time like an old, old man. He was tired, and he was hurting, and he was angry at the world. *God!* he screamed inside himself. *Bring my boys back! Bring them back alive!*

The Cado Swamp looked from the air like a vast, desolate, forbidding place. The mist rose from the surface in the early light, and the place seemed for all the world like the roof of hell, the fires smoldering underneath sending up smoke plumes. It stretched endlessly in every direction all the way to the horizon. Looking for the wreckage of a plane in this place was like looking for a needle in a haystack. But it was down there somewhere, that much was sure, and Ray was going to find it.

The air vibrated with the noises of at least ten planes and choppers as they criss-crossed methodically over their various sectors of the swamp. In the lead copter, Ray and Earl McCready sat up front directing the search. The planes zoomed by, making low passes over the soggy wasteland, and the copters hovered, circling in ever wider arcs.

As the lead copter hovered over an area thick

with brush, Ray gave a sudden start. His body straightened as he looked down into the shimmering mist. Forcing the throttle, he dove in low for a closer look. As they came down, Earl saw what Ray was looking at. Three clumps of brush were arranged below them appearing as though someone could have placed them there. But someone hadn't. Those bushes were put there by God, and both Earl and Ray knew it. Earl shook his head dubiously. In his opinion, there wasn't much hope of finding them alive. They were flying so low now that Earl could see the crocodiles snapping fiercely at them, furious at the intrusion, and backing off as they threatened with their jaws. Vines drooped from moss-bound trees, and birds flew in flocks of thousands.

Ray's face fell. His reserves of hope were beginning to run dry. Nevertheless, he forced himself to concentrate on the task at hand, grim as its final results might be. He pulled the chopper down even further, away from the other search craft. They were passing over a heavily forested area with a soggy clearing or a small patch of reed-covered bog here and there. Suddenly something white flashed from between the tops of two trees. Ray's heart leapt almost out of his chest as he brought the chopper in for a closer look.

There it was—broken neatly in two by its passage through the trees. Ray saw no trace of fire; apparently the craft hadn't burned. On the other hand, there were no signs of life, no movement down below. Then Ray caught his breath—about twenty feet beyond the nose of the plane, laid out in a patch where the trees parted exposing the ground below, were three bright yellow seat covers, with a fourth bent at an angle. Together they formed an arrow! Ray's eyes followed in the indicated direction, and there, on a swampy hillock a hundred yards away, Ray could see three small plumes of smoke rising among the mists, spiraling straight upward—three small fires! Ray burst out smiling, his face beaming, and he let out with a rebel yell as the sun burned through the mists revealing a miracle. They were alive!

Jock held the phone in his trembling hand and his eyes filled with tears. As he listened to Ray, his face gradually relaxed into a broad, deep smile. How grateful he felt toward the young man who was his ranch foreman. If Ray had been his son, Jock could not have loved him more than he did at that moment.

"And where was it that you actually found them?" he asked, more to keep Ray on the phone than for any other reason.

Ray detailed the final moments of the search for him. "Old J.R. had those three fires burning just like you said he would, Jock."

The old man nodded, gratified that his son's training had done some good. "Well thank God for that," he whispered. "All right, Ray, you've done good. Now bring my boys back home." There was a slight pause while Jock swallowed hard. "I'm grateful to you Ray," he concluded. "More than I can say." Gently, lovingly, he replaced the receiver on its cradle.

Jock went from the study into the living room where the women were waiting, knowing he was on the phone with Ray. As he crossed the hall, he reflected smugly for a moment that, for a change,

he was the one with the information. As he entered
the room, all the women rose as one, dread painted
clearly on all their faces. But at the sight of Jock's
beaming smile, they relaxed instantly. "They're
alive!" he boomed. "They're not even hurt!"

Sue Ellen rushed to him, as if not quite able to
believe the good news. "J.R.?" she asked.

"Both of them, Sue Ellen," Jock replied. "They
made it."

Pam wanted to rise into the air and fly, but
instead, her body, weak with exhaustion and
stress, collapsed back onto the sofa, and she
laughed heartily, all the nervousness exploding in
gales of hilarity. "It's all over . . . it's over . . ." she
kept repeating. Lucy ran to embrace her, smiling
from ear to ear.

"Johnnie's injured," Jock added, "but it's
nothing too serious. Nothing to worry about, he
said." Jock reached out his arms to hold Miss Ellie.
"Ray's gonna bring them back home, Miss Ellie,"
he said, hugging her fiercely. They were reprieved,
they were blessed, they were whole again.

The sun was high in the sky when the ranch car
finally made its triumphant way down the drive
toward the house. As it drove into the car park and
came to a stop, the front door burst open and the
women came pouring out onto the veranda. They
stood there, almost as if afraid to go any farther lest
the car be empty of its treasure—but Bobby and
J.R. got out, looking somewhat disheveled and
disoriented. They were obviously all right aside
from a cut or a bruise here and there and some
ripped clothing. At the sight of her husband safe
and sound, Pam launched herself like a missile

across the front yard to his waiting arms, laughing and crying all at once. They embraced as if they were all there was in the world, as if they would never let go of each other again, no matter what happened.

At the same time, Sue Ellen ran to J.R. But as she did so, she could not help hesitating when she reached him. After all that had happened, were things going to be different now? Or would they lapse back into the intolerable conditions that had almost driven her into another man's arms? The two of them stood there, not moving for quite some time, frozen in uncertainty. Finally it was J.R. who opened up his arms to embrace his wife. She moved into the embrace like a wounded bird, clinging to him, wanting so much for him to love her . . .

Now Miss Ellie moved forward to embrace each of her sons in turn. For her it was her very life which had been returned to her, no more, no less. Looking into their eyes, she felt whole again, and completely happy, unconcerned for the moment about the petty trials and tribulations that seemed to dog the Ewing clan.

Jock emerged from the house having held back long enough to allow the women their moments with the boys. Surveying the scene in front of him, he felt strangely distanced from the others. Once again securely in control of his emotions, he stood silently for a moment before striding slowly down the steps and walking toward his sons. He was trying, in his way, to make this extraordinary day just a normal one, a normal reunion between father and sons who hadn't seen each other in, say, a week. But as he looked at them, those men who were his sons, who were everything in the world to him, he could not stop himself from breaking into a big grin.

Embarrassed at his own show of emotion, he tried to cover with a little joke to break the ice. "I guess you boys cooked this whole thing up just to get out of a meeting with Ben Deering, huh?" he said, his eyes twinkling.

Bobby looked at his father, and then at his big brother. "We have J.R. to thank, Daddy. He saved our lives. When the plane hit the ground, Johnnie was pinned in his chair and I was blacked out for three solid hours. J.R. got us out of there and pulled us to shelter. It was he who set out the signals . . . he did it all." For once there was genuine and deep respect in Bobby's voice for his brother. He looked at him proudly, the way he used to when they were kids.

But J.R. did not return his brother's gaze. He was looking at his father, the man who was God to him. "I didn't forget, Daddy," he said softly, his eyes lit up with pride, his face glowing and innocent as it must have been once.

Jock moved forward to him, "No, you didn't son. You sure didn't. I'm proud of you, boy. You done good—real good."

J.R. blinked, touched by the blessing he had been given. His father's approval was more precious to him than anything. Jock hugged him tightly, and J.R. felt whole, more whole than he had felt in years. His daddy loved him. His daddy was proud of him. That's all that mattered in the world.

Jock embraced Bobby next, and the three of them walked back to the house together, three men bound by love. Ellie watched them go. When they had disappeared into the house, she turned to look at her daughters-in-law and her grand-daughter. "I love seeing them like that, together, and you like this, together. Maybe all our troubles are behind us now. Maybe now we can be a real family together."

Sue Ellen flinched. "I don't know what you're referring to, Miss Ellie," she said, all aflutter. "Why, aren't we always a family? We're all Ewings, after all . . ." She started for the house. "I'd better go in and see if J.R. wants me for anything." And she disappeared through the door.

"J.R. doesn't want her for anything," muttered Lucy. "He never does."

Miss Ellie looked at her reprovingly. "Stop talking like that, Lucy!" she demanded.

Lucy looked at the ground, abashed. "I didn't mean anything by it, Grandma," she said, as she started into the house.

Bobby stepped out onto the porch wondering what had become of his wife. "Hey, what are you doing out here?" he chided her. "All the action's inside!"

"Keep your shirt on, big boy!" she answered playfully, and, running to his arms, they went in together.

Alone now, Miss Ellie breathed deeply of the Texas air, perfumed with the smell of livestock and wildflowers. Life was good, she thought to herself. And in the blind joy of the moment, Ellie Ewing was convinced that the good times would stay with them forever.

Chapter Seven

Six weeks passed. The early buds of the Texas spring blossomed in the warmth of the powerful sun, and the flowers bloomed everywhere. Birds felt their blood run warm inside their veins and began flocking north from Mexico, swirling around the prairies, looking for places to nest and mate. Bees filled the air with their buzzing. It was a season to remember, a season of joyous, abundant rainstorms followed by triumphant sunshine for days on end, and the whole world seemed to rejoice in the weather.

At Southfork Ranch, the Ewing family, too, seemed to have been granted a reprieve. The boys were back; they were alive and happy. The near brush with death seemed to have given everybody a deeper appreciation of their bounty; and for a while, things were unusually happy to the point where Miss Ellie began to believe very strongly that they would stay that way forever, and that the plane crash had been a blessing in disguise after all.

In the early morning light, the big house stood blazing white in the sun. Over in the corrals, the family horses were groomed within an inch of their lives. They pranced gaily, celebrating the warmth of the day as it arrived, rejoicing in the touch of their hooves on the sweet, soft, moist earth.

Jock Ewing watched them, wondering how many new foals they would produce for him this year. He felt sure that there would be many, more than in any previous year. The beauty of this spring would surely make them full of desire for each other with the yearning to bring new life into this beautiful world. Come to think of it, he would not have been at all surprised if this was the year in which he would be presented with his first grandson. While Sue Ellen and J.R. continued to be cool to each other, in spite of all the natural forces at work, Pam and Bobby seemed more in love than ever. Surely, having gotten pregnant once before, Pam would soon conceive again. He watched their faces often to search for signs in their eyes and smiles.

Breathing in deeply, Jock felt at perfect peace with himself. In every direction his land spread out before him in golden waves of grass and brush, and the trees swayed sensually in the breeze. He was truly a lucky man. Even his own health was better, and that made all the difference in the world in his attitude.

After one last look around, he turned and headed for the patio. Miss Ellie was setting out breakfast, hoping to beat the bees who rarely showed their faces before nine in the morning, being too full of nectar from the day before. She handed her husband his daily glass of orange juice and his pills.

"My goodness, Jock," she remarked with obvious pleasure, "you certainly are becoming an early riser again!"

Jock laughed. "Yeah, I guess I am at that, Ellie," he agreed. "Bein' able to get around sure feels good. I'm beginning to get the feel of the ranch again."

Miss Ellie smiled. "My father was like that . . . always up early. He was a quiet man, didn't talk much. I guess he liked to feel things and keep them to himself."

"Well," Jock replied dubiously, "I don't know about keeping things to myself, but I do like the ranch. I want to be getting back to it soon now."

There was a sudden clattering down the stairs, and then the back door banged open revealing Bobby, late and in a hurry, the tail of his suit jacket flying behind him, his car keys already poised in his hand. He quickly kissed his mother and wished her and Jock a good morning. Miss Ellie offered him coffee, but he declined. "Don't have time today, Momma," he apologized. "I'm flying to Austin this morning for a noon meeting." Turning to his father to give a quick explanation, he added. "I'm showing these plans to Joe Morris, and . . ." His voice trailed off as he realized he had left the house without the vital plans. He grinned sheepishly at his own carelessness, and, shaking his head, made for the door.

He nearly collided with Pam, also on her way to work, who was holding an architect's drawing tube in her hands. Handing them to her husband, she smiled wryly. "I had a funny feeling these weren't mine," she quipped.

"All right, all right," Bobby said, embarrassed.

"I was just on my way to pick them up. You don't have to rub it in, wise guy." They nuzzled each other playfully and kissed. "See you later, sweetheart," said Bobby, as he took off for the garage.

Pam watched his retreating figure for a moment, and then stole a quick look at her watch. She, too, had better get a move on, if she wanted to get to work on time. By way of a greeting to Jock and Ellie, she said, "You know, I'm starting to miss those days before I went to work, when my life consisted of sitting around here and drinking iced coffee."

Jock raised his eyebrows at her remark. He had never felt at home with women holding down jobs, especially not Ewing women. As far as he was concerned, Pam's "career" was a temporary thing until she got tired of pretending she needed the money, or until she got pregnant and got down to the real work of a Ewing woman—raising the next Ewing generation. "Had it with your job, Pam?" he asked off-handedly.

Pam was aware of the tone in his voice, but it didn't bother her, secure in her work and in her position in the family as she had become. She felt she could handle the pressure better than before. "No, actually I love my work," she replied honestly. "It's just that it's inventory time this week, and all the cheap help has to be in by nine. Cheap help meaning me, of course."

Suddenly there was another commotion from inside the house, and Lucy could be heard shouting in frustration, "Well, it's just plain stupid, that's all!"

And Sue Ellen's reply told the family outside

that the argument was with her. "Why Lucy, sweetheart," she replied, barely concealing her annoyance with the girl, "I thought I told you I don't mind doing it for you. I enjoy it in fact."

Pam made a face in reaction to the voices, as if to say, "Well! Isn't somebody grouchy today!" and headed for her car waving good-bye to Jock and Ellie.

"I don't care if you do enjoy it!" Lucy shot back. "I happen to be as good a driver as anyone in this house, and I think it's high time that I had a car of my own!" As she said this, she emerged onto the patio followed by a somewhat distressed Sue Ellen. "Mornin' everybody," she said cheerfully enough to show that her annoyance with Sue Ellen was as much to get a rise out of her as anything else.

Sue Ellen, for her part, seemed genuinely threatened by Lucy's show of independence. It was as if, feeling herself a slave of her husband, she resented anyone else's independence. "If your Uncle J.R. feels you're old enough and mature enough to have a car of your own, I'm sure he'll buy you one. Until then, you'll have to drive with me."

"I don't see why J.R. gets to decide when I get a car," Lucy pouted. Turning to her grandfather, knowing she had him wrapped around her little finger, she cooed, "Granddaddy, don't you agree that I'm ready for a car of my own?"

Knowing that Jock would not be able to resist Lucy's manipulations, and wanting to spare Sue Ellen any further damage to her already fragile ego, Miss Ellie interrupted. "Leave your grandfather alone, Lucy," she commanded. "It's bad enough he spoils you rotten. I won't have you going to him as a court of last resort." Her voice was stern.

"All right, then," said a disappointed Lucy, "I'm going to ask J.R. about it." Not much chance of manipulating J.R. the way she did Jock, she was thinking, but she might be able to bother him enough so that he gave her the car just to keep her out of his hair. She started back into the house, but Sue Ellen stopped her.

"Your Uncle J.R. is not feeling well this morning, Lucy," she said, a slight quaver in her voice. "He's a bit under the weather. Maybe you'd better save your request for another day."

Lucy grinned knowingly at her aunt. "Old J.R. get drunk again last night?" she winked. "Boy, Sue Ellen, I really feel for you. It must be an awful strain . . ."

Sue Ellen flushed beet red. Fanning herself with her hand as she checked to see what the others had made of Lucy's remark, she hissed, "Lucy, really. Where is your respect for your uncle? You've been brought up right, you should know better than to be so fresh."

Lucy put her chin in her hand, as if considering what Sue Ellen had said. "You know, Sue Ellen, I believe you're right. I'll have to work on that." She grinned wickedly, pleased at the impact of her little thrust. "Well, Auntie, if we're going, we'd best be on our way, hadn't we?"

Furious, Sue Ellen said a quick good-bye to the others and marched off. Lucy followed her with a wink for her grandparents when Sue Ellen wasn't looking.

Jock and Ellie could not help smiling at Lucy's mischief. Not only was the girl as blunt as an old knife, but she always seemed to be right on target with her venom. "I think Lucy takes after your side of the family," said Jock wryly.

"Oh, I don't know," Miss Ellie mused. "I think she's got at least a little Ewing in her, too. At least half, in fact . . ."

Jock laughed. "Well, what if she has?" he demanded. "We've got our good side too, you know." And leaning over, he gave his wife a playful peck on the cheek.

As Pam walked down the street with her co-workers, Jean and Marie, the two other girls could barely contain their excitement. They were thrilled that Pam had desired their friendship. A woman of her power and influence didn't have to work at all, let alone associate with the common people. But Pamela Ewing was not at all pretentious, and she really was likeable at that. When she had invited them to lunch, they had nearly jumped out of their skins with pleasure. They had assumed they would be going to one of Dallas' posher restaurants, and they were right about that.

"I don't know, Pam," Jean was saying as they walked. "It makes no sense to me. If Bobby Ewing were my husband, I wouldn't be working at all . . . I'd be laying in bed till at least ten o'clock . . . at night, that is!" She dissolved into giggles of laughter.

Pam laughed, too. She really did like Jean, although she wished she wouldn't harp so on her money.

"I might never get out of bed at all," Marie added.

Or harp on her marriage, Pam thought.

"Actually," Pam replied, "I did think that's how

I'd feel about it, but after I got married, things changed. You get bored silly after a few weeks of that sort of stuff."

Jean shook her head in amazement. "You mean you'd rather put tags on dresses and take inventory for a living?"

"Well, it's not exactly what I had in mind, but it is work. And another thing I like about it is that it drives all the Ewings crazy. That alone makes it worth all the effort."

Again the girls dissolved in giggles. Pam was so funny. They were having the time of their lives. Not that they knew what she meant by her cryptic remark, but she sure was neat.

L'Entrecote was a four star restaurant with prices to match. Romantic in its atmosphere, with violins and harps sounding in the background, it was quiet and romantic even at its busiest. Famous as a rendezvous for lovers, especially of the secret kind, it was quite a treat for the shopgirls at The Store to be taken there. As they entered they were disappointed to see an impossibly long line in front of them. A harried hostess was doing an excellent job of explaining to the impatient would-be patrons why they would just have to wait. The girls looked at Pam in dismay sensing that they would not get to eat at this famous place after all. But Pam merely gave them a small, satisfied smile and approached the hostess who smiled broadly when she saw Pam.

"Mrs. Ewing! What a pleasant surprise to see you here!"

Pam knew that reservations were a must at L'Entrecote, but she ignored the unwritten rules made for mere mortals and simply asked if the hostess could find them a table for three.

As if by magic, the hostess said, "Of course I can, Mrs. Ewing. Will you and your party follow me please?"

Pam motioned to the astonished Jean and Marie, and they made their way past the annoyed ranks of waiting patrons—not so much annoyed as resigned to the fact that certain people had certain privileges which they could never aspire to.

"It sometimes does help to be a Ewing," Pam admitted, almost embarrassed by her power.

Suddenly Pam stopped in her tracks. She had noticed something, seen somebody, whom she had never in her life expected to see in such a place as this. Turning to her friends she told them to go on ahead without her, she would meet them at the table in a minute or two. Obligingly, the girls went on, looking around them at the impossible opulence and elegance of the place.

Pam headed for the corner where her brother Cliff was sitting alone at a table for two looking ill at ease in his seldom used sport jacket and tie. The posh surroundings seemed to weigh on him like an unaccustomed burden, and he strained toward the door as if he were waiting for someone.

"Well, what do you know?" said Pam as she came up beside him. "Aren't we moving up in the world?"

Cliff turned, startled. Seeing that it was Pam, a funny little look crossed his face and then disappeared, replaced by his customary jaunty smile. "Pammy!" he cried, seeming for all the world pleased to see his sister, though Pam did wonder what that little curious look had meant.

"Cliff, you'd better watch your step," she warned him mockingly. "If people notice you eating in a place like this they're going to start wondering what you did with all your leftover campaign contributions." It was a joke of course. Pam knew very well that, having lost the election due to the Ewings' underhanded tactics, Cliff was burdened by a heavy debt. It made it all the more curious that he should be eating here, where even a cup of coffee was a strain on his pocketbook. "When you take *me* out to lunch, it's always tacos and beer."

Cliff laughed, playing along, and at the same time keeping one eye on the door expectantly. "Well, little sister, I don't have to impress you. You already know me well enough to be impressed. Some people have to be convinced of my sterling qualities, among them, as you well know, generosity." It was a joke at his own expense. Cliff was well-known, and, in fact, cultivated a reputation for being tight with a buck.

"Hey," he challenged her, "I thought common working girls weren't allowed in this place."

Pam grinned, understanding the double meaning. Jealous and disapproving of her Ewing name and wealth, Cliff was reminding her of her plebeian origins. She didn't mind, though. As far as she was concerned, she was still the same woman, though much better off now. "My, my," she remarked, teasing him, "you have changed, Cliff. As I recall common working girls used to be just your speed."

"They still are," he admitted, with a touch of pride in his own ability with the ladies. Looking at his watch, he said, "Well, it looks as if this time I've been stood up. How 'bout me buying your lunch since you're here anyway?" His eyes twinkled.

Pam had to laugh out loud, knowing as she did how much pain it would cause Cliff to foot the bill for his rich sister in a place like this. "This must be your lucky day, Cliff. It so happens I'm buying lunch for a couple of working girls from The Store—we're sitting right over there." She pointed out Jean and Marie, who waved back at her, smiling. "How 'bout a rain check on it? Tacos are okay."

"You got it!" He laughed, relieved.

Pam turned to rejoin her friends, took a couple of steps, and nearly bumped right into Sue Ellen. The two women exchanged surprised looks. Sue Ellen was wearing a dress that must easily have cost a thousand dollars, and she looked like a million. Even Pam's breath was taken away. But what was her sister-in-law doing here? She couldn't have been with J.R.—his tastes ran more to the steak and bourbon kind of joint, like the Cattleman's Club, and besides, he and Sue Ellen hadn't exactly been romantic with each other lately . . . Could it be . . .?

"Why Pamela!" Sue Ellen said, much too loudly. "What a surprise to see you here!"

"Hello, Sue Ellen," Pam replied, hesitantly. "I had no idea you were going to be in town today."

Sue Ellen's eyes shot this way and that. "Oh," she said off-handedly, "an old friend called me at the last minute and I just couldn't resist."

"I'm eating with a couple of friends from The Store," said Pam. "If you'd like to join us, you're welcome to . . ."

"Why, isn't that nice of you dear," gushed Sue Ellen, her face flushing, "but I've already eaten.

I'm just on my way out. In fact, if you don't mind, I'll take a rain check on it."

While the two ladies talked, Cliff stood behind them. Out of the corner of her eye Pam spotted him. "Oh . . . Sue Ellen . . . how rude of me. This is my brother, Cliff. I believe you two have met, haven't you?" Pam was referring to the recent election campaign, during which Cliff had engaged in a debate, chaired by Sue Ellen in her capacity as Social Director of the Daughters of the Alamo. Sue Ellen had seemed to be charmed by Cliff at the time, Pam recalled. Now, however, in the posh surroundings of the restaurant, Sue Ellen seemed anything but friendly toward Cliff.

Cold as she had been to Pam, her manner grew even colder when he was introduced. "Yes, we have met before," she muttered, nodding tiredly.

"It's always nice to run into you, Mrs. Ewing," Cliff said, in a much nicer tone than Sue Ellen's, but still a little stiffly for him, Pam thought.

"Yes . . . well . . ." Sue Ellen made to leave, then stopped, realizing she had not properly dismissed herself. There was an uncomfortably long pause during which no one seemed able to say anything. Pam thought she saw a brief flush come into Sue Ellen's face.

"Ahem," Sue Ellen finally managed to make a sound. "Well, I hope you have a nice lunch, Pamela . . . good-bye, Mr. Barnes . . ." And with that, she quickly made for the exit.

Cliff and Pam stared at each other for a moment. "My, my." Pam smiled. "Wasn't that a warm little hello!"

Cliff shrugged. "I guess she's not real high on us Barneses, huh?"

Pam slapped him playfully on the hand. "Why, Cliff," she reminded him, "I'm a Ewing these days, remember?" Reaching over to kiss him on the cheek, she whispered, "So long, brother. See y' around, huh?" Waving to him over her shoulder, she wove her way between the tables until she reached her friends. Cliff watched her back until she was quite far away, and then he turned to stare in the other direction, the one in which Sue Ellen had gone.

Chapter Eight

In the old section of Austin, where Bobby had spent many wonderful days and nights lobbying the state legislature on Ewing Oil's behalf, stood the offices of Morris Enterprises, the firm of Joe Morris, architect and developer.

Years ago when Joe Morris had been just a young man of promise, Jock Ewing had hired him to design the Ewing building, and he had been close to the Ewings ever since. When Bobby decided to get into the construction business, it was Joe Morris he had gone to first for advice and ideas. The older man had been quite a bit of help to him, and now Bobby was approaching him with another set of plans, these drawn up by a young Dallas architect of promise, the master architect of the next generation.

But Joe Morris had other things on his mind. He did like the plans and was not equivocal in his praise of them. In fact he thought he could sell them in the future. But he was on to something else much bigger, much more interesting, and he wanted Bobby to sit down and talk about it.

"I don't know if you've ever heard of Faraday, Marshall and Mathis. Have you, Bob?"

Bobby thought for a moment. He hadn't heard of them, though the name did sound familiar.

"Well, let me tell you a little something about them to give you a better idea." Joe stood up and began pacing his office as he spoke. It was just something he did when he was hot on an idea. It made him think better. "They operate out of Boston, but they cover a whole lot more ground than that," he explained. "In fact, they just about cover the entire Northeast corridor. They're into a lot of different things. Mutual fund families, insurance, personal and corporate investing . . . the whole feedlot."

Bobby raised his eyebrows. Even a Ewing could be impressed with that kind of power. "Sounds like solid, Mayflower money."

"You got it," Joe continued. "Well, for two hundred years or so they've stayed solid as a rock, not moving. Now, suddenly, they're ready to expand. Maybe the news reached them that there are more than thirteen states now. But the big news is they're intending to build a branch in the Southwest. Beginning to get the big picture?"

Bobby's eyes were aglow, excited by the prospect. "If they're gonna build in the Southwest, it'd be a shame if they didn't settle on Dallas. After all, where better?"

Joe Morris raised his hands in the air as if to say, of course! "I'd been thinking about some of that prime land the Ewings own around town . . ."

Bobby reflected for a moment. He found it a

useful thing to do at such moments. He searched himself for anything that didn't feel right about it. "Wouldn't a company as old and stuffy and reputable as this one want to do business with another old, established firm out here? One of the old, famous building firms?"

Joe shook his head. "That's just it, Bobby, don't you see? They want to change their image . . . pull in more young investors. That's why they're expanding in the first place. Think about it. It makes sense, doesn't it?"

Bobby nodded. He had to agree. "How soon can we get together with them?" he wanted to know.

"Well, I've already done some legwork," confided Joe proudly. "They'll be out here on the seventeenth . . . that's two weeks from Saturday."

"Two weeks, huh?" mused Bobby. An idea was coming to him, an idea like those he'd had to come up with when he was a lobbyist. "Why don't we have them come out to Southfork, throw a big party for them? You know, impress them with our Texas hospitality."

Joe laughed in agreement. He had been to Southfork Ranch many times. If the big boys from back east were not impressed with Southfork's size, if it didn't show them beyond a shadow of a doubt that they were dealing with one of the pillars of the community, even of the whole state of Texas, then he would eat his ten-gallon hat. "I think it's a great idea, Bobby," he said, as Bobby rolled up the plans he had brought with him and slid them back into their tube. "Let's go ahead with it."

"Fine," said the younger man, capping the tube

with a flourish of contentment. "I'll take care of all the preparations."

"Good," Morris said. "Say, don't go so fast. Let me take you to dinner—coupla good steaks?"

Bobby shook his head, extending his hand to Morris. "Thanks, Joe, but no thanks. I really have got to head back home. Dinner'll be on me when you get to Dallas, how's that?"

"Even better!" Morris laughed. "See you then. I'll be calling you."

Bobby left the office, full of confidence in the success of his construction business, proud of the fact that he had started it himself and built it himself; he was completely unaware of the trouble that had just begun to brew.

The Store was just closing and all the workers were coming down the aisle headed for the front door double file, chatting with each other, their work day over. Pam made her way among them, accepted and accepting, for the moment unaware of the great distance put between herself and the rest of them by all the money she had married into. From behind her, she heard the voice of Liz Craig calling her name.

"Wait a second, Pam!" she cried. Pam stepped out of the parade, waiting by a mannequin wearing the latest in summer swimwear, as Liz caught up to her, and together they left the building and headed for the parking lot.

"How's everything been for you?" Liz asked off-handedly.

Pam smirked. "Oh, just great," she replied sardonically. "I'm becoming a whiz at markdowns lately."

Liz had to laugh. Pam was her special friend and protégé, and she knew what an intelligent, capable woman she was. Liz would have started her out at an executive position, but Pam had insisted she work her way up like anybody else, obviously sensitive to her own great wealth, and anxious to make her way on her own in spite of it.

"I guess being a sales clerk isn't all you thought it would be," Liz joked.

"Well, to tell you the truth," Pam confided, coming to a halt by her car, "I did want to start small, but I didn't think it would be so very microscopic, if you know what I mean."

Liz knew exactly what she meant. "I have great things in store for you, Pam . . . you'll see. Now that I see you're ready, it won't be long."

Pam caught her breath. "When can I hear about all this?" she asked eagerly.

"Not yet," Liz replied. "But it won't be long, you can count on that. I promise you. Sometime very soon, I'll have some good news for you." She patted Pam on the arm, and turned to go. "See you in the morning, bright and early!"

Pam watched her go, feeling that someone listened to her prayers after all. Good things did come to those who wait. And God knows she had waited long enough. With all the pressure from the Ewings about working, it would be a lot easier to hold her own with an executive position, something that would earn, if not their respect, at least a respite from their disdain.

In the Southfork dining room, the entire family was gathered. It was a good feeling to have them all together again, thought Miss Ellie, remembering the evening six weeks before when the boys had been missing and she'd thought they'd never be coming back again.

Now, as Raoul picked up the empty dinner plates, and Teresa came around to pour coffee for everyone, the conversation broke up into little groups.

Bobby turned to Pam, to tell her about his day. "Joe Morris liked the plans, but there was something else he wanted to talk to me about . . . something really big, as it turns out. It would be quite a project."

Pam nodded appreciatively, but did not ask him to elaborate. She was too full of her own good news. "Liz Craig called me aside after work and told me I'm on the verge of a promotion!"

Bobby smiled, but his eyes reflected not pleasure but worry. "Does that mean you're gonna be working more overtime?" he wanted to know.

Pam shrugged, trying to maintain a good attitude. "Don't know yet," she answered. "We'll have to see what tomorrow brings."

On their side of the table, J.R. was asking Sue Ellen whether she'd managed to get to Harvey's to pick up the new suit they were altering for him.

"I sure did, darlin'," she said. "I happened to be down that way for lunch, so it was no problem to pick it up."

"Good, good." He nodded. "And I don't suppose you got a tie to go with it, did you?"

Sue Ellen smiled her most self-satisfied smile. She was a wife to beat all wives, and she was letting him know it. "Red, with a little black stripe . . . a dress shirt, too."

J.R. patted her on the wrist. Having attended to

that little business, he raised his voice to carry across to Bobby's side of the table. "'Scuse me, brother," he interrupted, "but there's a favor I'd like to ask of you, if you don't mind."

"Sure thing, J.R., ask away," Bobby replied, foolishly agreeing before he had even heard what the favor was.

"I know you've been out in the field a lot, what with all your big construction deals . . ." J.R. was delivering a roundabout dig. He had never liked the idea of Bobby's going into business for himself, fearing that his brother would do well and show him up. Jock mostly agreed with J.R. on the subject, feeling that Bobby's proper place was in the family business, Ewing Oil. While that was the last thing J.R. wanted, he was not above taking a joust at his brother in front of his father. Besides, he really did need a favor from him. "Anyhow, bein' away so much," he went on, "I don't guess you're aware of all the lobbying the independent oilmen are doing up in Washington. There's a lot at stake for us right now."

Bobby rolled his eyes. "I may be busy, J.R., but I knew that, all right."

"Did you now?" J.R. said, feigning amazement. "Well, since you understand the importance of the lobbying effort we're engaged in, you won't mind holding down the fort at Ewing Oil while I'm gone."

Sue Ellen looked up, startled. "Gone?" she asked. "You mean you're going to Washington?" It was inconceivable to her that, as distanced as they had become of late, he had failed to tell her of his trip. She did not expect to be invited to come with him, but at least he could have informed her!

"Yes, darlin'," he smiled sweetly. "Just made the arrangements today, in fact."

Having explained the surprise announcement to Sue Ellen, at least to his own satisfaction, J.R. turned to Bobby, once more all business. "It's real important, Bobby, that everything goes the way we want at this legislative session. I'm sure you understand."

Bobby understood all right, but J.R.'s request could not have come at a more inconvenient time for him. "Look, I'd love to, J.R., you know that, but right now I've got half a dozen important things going, and I don't see how I could . . ."

J.R. raised his hand, stopping him. "Bobby, correct me if I'm wrong," he said, shaking his head in mock confusion, "but I was under the impression that your little business venture was merely a sideline. You know as well as I do that Ewing Oil is the company that matters in this family." It was incontrovertible.

"Yes, that's true, all right," Bobby was forced to agree. "But I can't postpone some of the meetings I've got planned for this week. They're too important!"

"Well," shrugged his brother, "have them come and meet with you at the office."

Jock had been listening silently while the two brothers hassled it out, but all the while he had been thinking of another solution. "Listen here," he spoke up. "I think that after all the years I spent building that company I know enough about it to keep it afloat for a few days without sending us all to the poorhouse."

Miss Ellie raised her eyebrows dubiously. "Do you really think you should, Jock? You're still recovering, remember?" she warned.

Jock grew annoyed, as he always did when Miss Ellie reminded him of his frail health. "Aw, look, now, I'm not gonna be breakin' rocks, am I? I'm gonna be sittin' behind a desk, mindin' the store, is all! I don't know why everybody makes such a fuss every time I decide to move my butt out of a chair!"

"Look," said Bobby, anxious to accommodate his mother's worries. "I suppose I could juggle some of my meetings and still get it done."

"Don't you worry about it, son," his father motioned him off. "I'll take care of it. It should be fun for me . . . probably do me a world of good to have to use my brain a little again on something besides backgammon."

J.R. gave them both a warm smile. "Why, that's very good of you, Daddy. I guess that about takes care of everything. I can go to Washington with full faith that Ewing Oil is in the best of hands."

Sue Ellen had remained still as she silently calculated, her gaze turned inward. "What time does your plane leave, darlin'?" she asked.

"Ten thirty."

"Fine," she said, smiling and putting down her coffee cup. "I'll drive you to the airport myself."

J.R., far from being pleased by her offer, drew his lips back into a grimace of discomfort. "Uh . . . that's all right, sweetie, there's no need for you to take the trouble . . ."

"Oh, no trouble at all," Sue Ellen insisted gaily. "It'll be fun for me. We'll have the chance to spend some time together and chat. What with you bein' so all-fired busy lately, you and I have hardly seen each other."

It was Sue Ellen's turn to get in a dig. The whole family was painfully aware of J.R's tendency to "work" late evenings, sometimes staying out all night. If they thought about what was probably going on, they didn't say anything out of respect for the couple's privacy. Nevertheless, Sue Ellen had phrased her offer in such a way that there was no way J.R. could turn it down, not with the whole family in attendance. He gave the only graceful reply possible under the circumstances—he agreed.

The crickets were chirping madly, singing their mating song, as the grandfather clock in the hall struck midnight. Sue Ellen crept stealthily down the stairs, carefully avoiding the places that would creak if she put her weight on them. Her diaphanous nightgown billowed about her as she descended the stairs, silhouetting her ample feminine curves against the white wall behind her. There was an indefinable aura about her, so that anyone who had come upon her would have been shocked to see a side of Sue Ellen strangers never saw—an incredibly passionate, boldly sensual side. Slinking over to the door that led to the study, she slid it open and went inside, closing it silently behind her like a master spy on a mission of great importance and secrecy. Carefully, she picked up the phone and dialed, looking over her shoulder constantly and listening for approaching footsteps which never came.

The phone rang once on the other end and a voice said "Hello?" It was a masculine voice.

"Hello, darling," she answered, her voice husky with desire. "I know it's late, but I couldn't call till now . . . he's just fallen asleep this minute . . . that's right . . . listen—I called to tell you some wonderful news—he's going to Washington in the morning. He'll be gone for a few days . . ."

The voice on the other end of the line said something in a low, conspiratorial tone.

"Certainly I'm sure," she replied, unable to suppress a little giggle of pleasure. "I'm putting him on that plane myself—I made him an offer he couldn't refuse . . . there's no problem there . . . so I'll see you tomorrow, my love . . . we'll have lots and lots of time together at last . . . I can't wait . . . goodnight." She placed the phone back carefully and stared off into space, allowing the warm vibrations to course through her excited body as she smiled in secret anticipation.

The gray-green Mercedes with the license number EWING 3 turned off the highway and into the Dallas-Ft. Worth Airport, a gigantic place stretching in every direction as far as the eye could see, a fitting airport for the greatest city in Texas. Sue Ellen, behind the wheel, drove to the departure ramp and pulled up in front of a line of taxis dropping off their fares.

J.R. leaned over to her and gave her a chaste little peck on the cheek. "You have a nice time now, hear?" he said cheerfully.

"Oh, I will," she replied, a knowing smile on her face. "Hope you have a nice flight."

"I'm sure I will." He smiled. "I've been in enough plane wrecks for one lifetime."

On that macabre note, he grabbed his attache case and hopped out of the car. Sue Ellen stayed where she was until he disappeared inside the terminal. Then, satisfied that he was really on his way to Washington, she pulled away, her body aflame with eagerness.

At the front door of the plane, J.R. handed his boarding pass to the stewardess, placed his carry-on bag in the compartment provided for such parcels in the first class cabin, and made his way down the aisle to his seat. In the seat next to him was a smashing-looking redhead with long legs and well-manicured nails. She turned to J.R. and flashed him a big smile. He took her hand in his, and kissed her deeply on the mouth. "Judy," he said, "this is going to be some wonderful trip."

"Mmmm . ." she replied, her tongue licking her lips lasciviously. "You have no idea how I've been looking forward to this."

J.R. laughed a wicked little laugh. "It's gonna be even better when you look back on it darlin', you mark my words." They squeezed each other's hands as the plane left the ground and soared into the air.

Bobby proceeded into the office at a brisk pace. He was dressed, not in the three piece suit he used to wear when he was a part of Ewing Oil, but in work clothes and cowboy boots. Under his arm was a batch of architect's plans. Crossing to Connie's desk, he asked the receptionist if anybody needed him.

"Well," she said, leafing through her message pads, "there was a phone call from a Mr. Cooper at the bank."

"Okay," Bobby responded, making a mental note to call the banker back later, "anything else?"

"The plumbing contractor, Mr. Dixon, said he

needed to talk to you, but he was going to be out all day and said he'd call you later. Let's see, Mister Thomas from the plumbers' union . . ."

Bobby checked that one off, too, deciding to deal with Thomas at a later date.

"Oh, and Joe Morris called—urgent, he said you're to call him right away."

"Okay," Bobby assented, "I'll do that. Is Jock here yet?"

She nodded, pointing to J.R.'s office.

Bobby called back to her as he walked over that way. "Put in that call to Morris, will you, Connie? I'll take it in here." And with that he disappeared into the office.

Jock was ensconced behind J.R.'s desk, his feet up, leafing through some papers and looking out the window at the panoramic view of Dallas. Bobby greeted his father, but Jock merely grunted back at him.

"Why in the hell do you think your brother made such a big fuss over us filling in for him? Everybody who calls up says they want to talk to him and nobody else! It's no use at all my being here."

Bobby laughed, recognizing the problem from his own bitter experience. "If you remember, Daddy," he wagged his finger, "I told you J.R. ran a tight ship. He keeps things entirely to himself where Ewing Oil is concerned. When I was here, I was only allowed to talk to my secretary. My functions at meetings were to pour coffee and smile a lot, nod my head once in a while. That's why I'm in construction now."

Before Jock could offer a reply, the intercom buzzed on the desk and he reached for it. Bobby stopped him, putting up his hand. "That's a call for me, if I'm not mistaken," he said, and picked up the telephone. "Hello? Hi, Joe, Bobby here."

"Mornin', Bobby," Morris crowed. His mood was chipper, and the news was therefore obviously good. "I bring good news, cowboy."

Bobby laughed. "It wouldn't be about an old-line family of eastern blue-bloods and their green money, would it?"

"You're a good guesser, boy," said Morris. "I just talked to the principals in person . . . Mr. Harrison and Mr. Faraday. That's Faraday of Faraday, Inc., Faraday Enterprises, Faraday et cetera."

"All right, all right, I'm suitably impressed," Bobby said. "What's the word, Joe? Are they coming out to Dallas for a visit?"

"Weeelll, I told him you'd invited him out to the ranch for a party . . . mixing business and pleasure. Told him we'd show them around Dallas, with the emphasis on Southfork, one of the famous great ranches of Texas. He and the Missus are gonna come out for the party. And they're bringing a bunch of the decision-makers, too."

Bobby let out a whoop. If they came out to Southfork, he felt sure the deal was in his pocket. But Morris cautioned him. "They're lookin' forward to meeting you, Bobby, but listen—they're also lookin' forward to meeting your wife."

Bobby's face took on a quizzical expression. "Pam? I don't understand . . . what has she got to do with any of this?"

"Weeelll, you know how these blue-blooded Mayflower people are . . . they're real conservative . . . place as much emphasis on how a man conducts his personal life as on how he runs his business affairs. A *lot* of importance. What I'm saying is that Pam could be worth about half the deal to us."

Bobby smiled, confident. "Don't worry about a thing, then, Joe," he said. "If it's up to Pam, the deal is in our pockets for sure."

"All right, if you say so, Bobby," said Morris. "I've never met the lady, but if you think she can do the job, I believe you."

"No sweat," Bobby assured him.

"Well, cowboy, see you next week, huh?"

"You bet." Bobby hung up and slapped his hands together in triumph. "Hey, Daddy!" he crowed to his father. "Do you remember that parcel of brushland you bought—north of Greenville?"

"I remember it all right," said his father, a disgusted look on his face. "I remember there wasn't a drop of oil on it. Dry as a good martini. I sure regretted that one, but you can't win 'em all."

"Well, Daddy," Bobby continued, sitting cross-wise on the desk, "looks like you won after all. I think we just struck gold on that land—and I don't mean black gold, either!"

Sue Ellen lounged luxuriously on the sofa surveying the small bachelor apartment, her negligee revealing more than it hid, her heart pounding furiously with excitement. Reaching into her purse, she drew out a small, beautifully wrapped package. "I bought you a little gift, my darling," she said, her voice raised to carry as far as the bathroom.

"Is that so?" came the man's voice, its tone romantic and earthy.

"You've probably forgotten the fact that it was

exactly six weeks ago—six weeks ago today, that we first . . . that I first came to your place." Taking her drink with her, she perched herself on the edge of the bed. "Darling," she cooed, "let me propose a little toast." Raising her glass high in the air above her radiant face, she said, "To my dear, sweet, thoughtful husband, J.R. Ewing, who has, for the first time in memory, done something genuinely nice for me . . . and for you. He's gone off to our nation's capital, to do whatever it is he does, or pretends to do . . . leaving us blissfully alone for three whole days of love, passion and romance."

"Now that's a toast worth drinking to," said Cliff Barnes, appearing at the bathroom door, his glass raised, his bathrobe hanging loose about his manly frame. He moved toward her and they clinked glasses, gazing longingly into each other's eyes. "To J.R. Ewing," he said, nibbling her earlobe, "long may he travel."

Chapter Nine

The morning sun reflected like a million shimmering gold coins off the surface of the pool as Pam's curvaceous figure cut its way through the water from the deep end to the shallow to complete her daily laps. She swam with her head mostly down, like the accomplished swimmer she was, and so she did not hear the banging of the patio door as Bobby came bounding out of the house in his bathing suit, ran over to the pool, and did a cannonball dive into the water coming up right by her side. The wave his impact made overwhelmed the unsuspecting Pam, who went under and came up gasping for air coughing up the water she had swallowed. "Would you quit that!" she cried, flailing around trying to catch her breath.

"Hey, did I even touch you?" he teased her playfully, splashing a little water her way.

"Ooooo . . . I hate you when you're this disgustingly happy!" She shook her fist at him.

"Oh, yeah? Who says I'm happy?" he

challenged her. "I happen to be on the verge of the biggest deal of my career, but that's no reason to be happy, is it?"

They made their way out of the pool, sparring playfully with each other like newlyweds. Picking up a couple of towels, they went over to a table where continental breakfast and coffee were elegantly laid out for them, courtesy of Raoul, with a little help from Teresa.

"You know," Pam said, as she buttered herself a croissant, "I've got to be out of here in five minutes. Gotta get dressed and go to work. My hair's all wet, too, thanks to you. And you've made me all nervous about this party I'm supposed to throw."

"Whoa, there, wait just a second. In the first place," said Bobby, "your hair was good and wet before I even got here. And why should you be nervous about the party—just because the whole deal is riding on your shoulders, that's no reason to get anxious."

Pam rolled her eyes. "Can't we be serious about this for a minute? I mean, I really am nervous about it."

Bobby sat her down and poured her some coffee. "Okay, let's be serious, but only for a minute. It isn't life or death, after all. It's not like you're a brain surgeon—one slip and that's it—it's a party, for God's sake . . . is that such a big deal?"

"Do you have any idea how many big parties I've thrown in my life?" she asked him. "If you guessed one, you're too high. I don't know the first thing about them!"

Bobby patted her on the head. "Well, then, isn't it lucky for you that there happens to be a resident

expert right here at Southfork. I'm sure that Sue
Ellen would be happy to give you the benefit of her
vast expertise on the subject—if you ask her, that
is . . ."

Pam thought for a moment. "It's true . . . she is
the queen of hostesses . . ."

"Problem solved," said Bobby, toasting her with
his coffee cup. "Now we're ready to tackle the
earthshaking problem of your wet hair!"

"Very funny, wise guy," she smirked. "I think
I'll try handling that one myself, without your help
or Sue Ellen's." Giving him a peck on the cheek
and a pinch on the arm, she got up and headed for
the house. Turning back, she said, "Sometimes it's
so awful being a Ewing . . . such a burden . . ."
Laughing, she disappeared inside the house.

Bobby looked after her and felt deeply gratified
that he had finally succeeded in making her happy
here at Southfork as one of the family. Finishing his
coffee, he got up and dove into the pool.

Sue Ellen stood alone in the entry hallway speaking
on the phone in a hushed tone. One hand held the
receiver, the other cupped it to mute her voice. She
kept turning her head this way and that to make
sure she was not being observed, and her eyes
darted quickly back and forth in all directions. She
did not feel guilty in the least. J.R. had given her
every reason to be unfaithful to him, and nobody
could blame her. Still, the stakes were very high for
her. If she should be found out, J.R. would
probably throw her out, and she would be alone
again, with nothing but the shirt on her back to
show for all her years of loyalty and sacrifice.

But the overwhelming feeling racing through her

was not fear, but excitement. She was in love again, in the grip of a flaming passion, and the need for secrecy only made the flame flare hotter and higher. She was walking a tightrope and loving every minute of it.

". . . When they asked where I was going, I told them an old friend of mine had come to town for a few days and I was taking her out to dinner . . ." she was saying, giggling mischievously as she spoke. "Meet me at four o'clock in the park by Lake Bachman, okay?" She listened to Cliff's reply, then added, "I'll bring the sandwiches and the wine, darling, you just bring your wonderful self . . ." Hearing his reply, she blushed deeply and dissolved into girlish laughter. "Now, now, we've got to eat sometime, or we'll burn up every calorie in our bodies!"

There was a footfall upstairs, then footsteps coming closer. Sue Ellen, alarmed, quickly whispered, "Four o'clock!" Then her tone changed completely as she said in a loud, formal voice, "All right, sir . . . when J.R. gets back from Washington I'll let him know you wanted to speak with him. I'm sure he'll be glad to hear you're in town. Good-bye." She hung up, looking up in time to see Pamela coming down the stairs dressed for work.

Seeing Sue Ellen, she called out, "Oh, hi! Could I talk to you for a minute, Sue Ellen?"

Sue Ellen's jaw tightened in fear. She wondered for a moment if Pamela had heard anything she shouldn't have. "Um . . . I'm kind of in a hurry, darlin' . . . could it possibly wait?"

Pam bit her lip, thinking. "Are you headed into town?" she asked.

Sue Ellen wasn't sure how to answer, but finally, after hesitating a bit too long, she admitted that she was.

"Good!" said Pam, smiling. "Let me buy you lunch . . . I have to talk with you about something important."

"Oh, look, dear, I'm going to be very busy today," Sue Ellen began.

"Yes, I realize that," said Pam, causing Sue Ellen to give a start, fearing once more that her secret had somehow been divined. "Even so," continued Pam, "I do need to talk to you."

Sue Ellen was beginning to panic. Whatever was the girl doing? If she knew, why didn't she just come out and say so? "Why don't we talk about it right now?" she asked, trying to force the issue.

But Pam shook her head. "I've got to get to work. Can we meet at, say, one? L'Entrecote?"

Sue Ellen made an exasperated face. It was the very restaurant where Pam had almost surprised her with Cliff. "Oh, all right. I'll be there."

Pam gave her a friendly smile and left. Sue Ellen looked after her. What did the girl know, she wondered. And what did she want from her?

Pam hurried down the street glancing at her watch. She was already ten minutes late for her appointment with Sue Ellen! What if she'd already left? Pam worried that Sue Ellen might be angry and refuse to help her. It took so little to antagonize her sister-in-law, and Pam was well aware of it.

Arriving at the restaurant at last, Pam approached the hostess. "Hi, Mrs. Ewing," the young woman greeted her, "your party has already arrived—may I take you to her?" Pam nodded appreciatively and followed behind her through the lunchtime crowd.

Sue Ellen sat at a table in the corner, the kind of table one sat at for intimate conversations. She had chosen it in case Pam wanted to talk about her secret. She sat there, sipping on a long, cool drink, something tall and heavy on the alcohol.

"I'm so sorry to be late, Sue Ellen, I hope you forgive me," Pam said as she sat down.

Sue Ellen eyed her testily, obviously annoyed, not only by Pam's lateness, but by the whole prospect of lunching with her. "You knew I had a lot to get done today, Pamela," she said. "You could at least have been prompt."

Pam apologized again, saying truthfully that she had gotten caught at a meeting and that she appreciated Sue Ellen giving her the time.

Sue Ellen snorted, not impressed. "You made it sound like—like something life or death," she said, holding her hand to her chest, thinking of that phone call to Cliff. "I felt I couldn't refuse." Now was the moment, she thought. If Pamela was out to blackmail her, she had just been given the invitation to lay her cards on the table.

But instead, Pamela said, "I need a favor from you, Sue Ellen—can you give me some advice?"

It was the last thing in the world Sue Ellen had expected to hear coming out of her sister-in-law's mouth. All day long she'd been preparing for the worst, making every innuendo fit her tortured imaginings until she'd worked herself into a worried frenzy. Now, all it had turned out to be was this! Sue Ellen's stomach released itself rapidly from the knot it had tied itself into, and she expelled a gust of air that came out sounding like a laugh of scorn but was in reality a laugh of sheer relief. "My advice?" she said shrilly. "Why, Pamela, you've never asked me for my advice in all the months we've known each other! You want my advice?"

"Yes," said Pamela again, realizing it was out of character for her. "In this case you're the unchallenged expert. You see, Bobby needs me to throw a big party at the ranch—on the seventeenth—that's less than two weeks away, and I don't know the first thing about how to do it."

Sue Ellen looked at her as if she was crazy, and burst out laughing, drawing looks from several of the other patrons. "You mean you asked me out here just to discuss a party? That's what was so important?" Sue Ellen gave such parties every few months, and to her they were the stuff of life, but she had done them so many times that they were nothing to her in terms of preparation, and she could not imagine why anyone but a complete moron would need help throwing one—it was as if someone had asked her how to breathe. She laughed not in mockery, but in relief. She still couldn't quite believe it. Maybe Pam still had something up her sleeve and was only doing all this to torture her . . . no, it couldn't be, she decided. Nevertheless . . .

"Pamela," she asked warily, "If it's all about this party, as you say, then why couldn't we have discussed it this morning? I don't understand why you engineered all this—" she gestured around her indicating the restaurant. "Is it really all that important to you?"

Pam lowered her head. She and Sue Ellen were so different. "To *me*, yes, Sue Ellen, in my life, this party is very important. I know it's only a party, but I've never thrown one in my life. I never cared about those things until I married Bobby and became a Ewing."

Sue Ellen was looking at her in a very funny way. It suddenly dawned upon Pam that she might have been misreading the whole situation. "Sue Ellen . . ." she said, slowly drawing out the words, "I get the feeling from the way you're acting that you thought I dragged you here to talk about something else entirely. What did you expect me to say?"

Sue Ellen snorted disdainfully. "Don't be silly. I had no idea what you were going to say! What do you think I am? A clairvoyant?" She laughed again. Then, realizing that she might be overreacting, she made haste to change the subject. "I'd be just delighted to help you plan your little party, Pamela." She paused to smile woodenly. "But I haven't got very much time. Here's what you do — you call my caterer . . ." She fished in her pocketbook for his card. Finding it, she extended it across the table. "He'll help you plan all the little touches you'll need to make your party a big success."

Pam stared at her. Sue Ellen was behaving very strangely, now that she thought of it. What was going on with her, Pam wondered? She thanked her for the card, apologizing again for bothering her, and then said, "Shall I call the waiter over? My treat, of course."

But Sue Ellen was somewhere else altogether, her mind miles away. She was gathering her things to go, sliding toward the open end of the booth. "Uh, Pam . . ." she said distractedly, "I think, if you don't mind terribly, I'd like to take a rain check

. . . I've been feeling kind of queasy lately . . . not at all like eating . . . excuse me, please."

Now that Pam looked at her, Sue Ellen's complexion did have a sort of greenish cast to it. "Sure, Sue Ellen," she said. "I really do thank you for helping me, and for taking the time."

Sue Ellen nodded and quickly left. Pam watched her back, and frowned perplexedly. What in the world was going on with Sue Ellen?

Jock stared out the window at the busy city below. The phone was in his hand, and he was talking long-distance. "J.R., that you?" he shouted. The connections these days are terrible, thought Jock. You would have thought they would make an exception for customers like Ewing Oil, but apparently the telephone company was a democratic institution, mistreating all its customers equally. "How is everything out there in D.C., boy?" he wanted to know. "I been here at the office all day and you haven't called in once . . . don't you think I deserve to know how the trip is goin'?"

On the other end of the line, J.R. sat in a large suite dressed only in a bathrobe, surrounded by the remains of a buffet luncheon and several empty bottles. "You know how it is, Daddy," he said consolingly. "I'm busy spreadin' around the three 'B's,' just like you taught me—booze, broads, and booty . . ."

"Good boy," Jock exclaimed, pleased that J.R. had given him some credit, like a good son should. "Got to make sure everyone stays happy and well-entertained." He laughed.

As J.R. talked, Judy emerged from the

bathroom and sashayed over to the wet bar to fix the two of them some drinks. As he spoke, she brought it to him, and sat down next to him as close as she could get.

"Yessir, Daddy, you always taught us that lobbying was a fine art, and by golly it is . . ." J.R. made a funny sound as Judy's skilled hands stroked his face, his chest, his arms. J.R. had trouble concentrating on his father.

"What's that you say, Junior?" Jock yelled into the phone. "The damn connection's so bad I can hardly hear a thing."

"Uh . . . don't you fret, Daddy. I'm loooookin' after the Ewings' interests—ooomnn!" There was a long pause on the other end of the line.

"I better say goodbye, Junior," said his father, "I'm hearing all sorts of noises . . ."

J.R. caught his breath long enough to say "Okay, Daddy—no news right now, but in this case no news is good news . . ." He exhaled deeply as Judy got busier. "Give my love to Sue Ellen and Mama." He hung up quickly and downed his drink in one swallow, then turned his full attention to the job at hand—a very pleasant job indeed.

Sue Ellen and Cliff walked slowly along the shore of beautiful Lake Bachman, holding hands like lovers, gazing off into the distance and breathing deeply of the scents of wildflowers. In the distance, small children sailed toy boats and couples rowed lazily on the lake. It was an idyllic scene, so unlike the rest of the city it was a part of, the city which went its workaday way while they strolled, walking more on air than on the path.

At least Sue Ellen was walking on air, but Cliff Barnes had his mind on other things. As they passed under the shade of a luxuriant weeping willow tree, he asked, without breaking stride or turning to her, "What's the purpose of J.R.'s trip to Washington?"

Sue Ellen shrugged, bored with J.R.'s continual business trips and meetings that always excluded her. "Oh, just what he's usually up to, I expect," she replied.

Now Cliff shot her a quick glance. "Interesting you should say that," he said. "Are you still so loyal to him that you keep his business secrets sacred?"

Sue Ellen felt vaguely annoyed. She wanted only to enjoy being together and in love. "I am never privy to J.R.'s machinations, Cliff. I keep telling you. Why won't you believe me?"

"Hmmm . . ." mused Cliff. "And if you were privy to some of his secrets? What then, Sue Ellen?"

She stopped walking for a moment. "Is that why you turned your irresistible charm on me, Mr. Barnes?" she asked, toying with him. "Did you really seduce me just to have me spy on my husband for you?"

Cliff put his hand on his chest as if he had been wounded, and said, in mock hurt, "How could you accuse me of something so ingenuous? In fact, my dear lady, it was the way you raise your eyebrows . . . but it is true that I am curious about what makes J.R. Ewing run."

"My dear Mr. Barnes," she smiled, affecting formality, "if I want to talk about J.R. Ewing, there are lots of people at home I can talk to about him.

That's not what I came here to discuss with you. It's the most unromantic thing I can think of, in fact."

Cliff saw that he had pressed too far and moved to make amends. Reaching down at the side of the path, he picked a handful of wildflowers and handed them to her, saying, "Then let's talk about love, shall we?" From the beaming smile on Sue Ellen's face, he knew he had done the right thing.

"Why thank you, sir," she said softly, smelling the fragrant blossoms. "To what do I owe the honor of this gift?"

Cliff smiled. "To the fact that they're free for the taking. I'm not exactly known as the last of the big-time spenders, you know."

Sue Ellen laughed and shook her head. One of the things she found most endearing about Cliff was his way of being crude and charming at the same time. He got away with the kind of gaucheness very few people could. "It's disgusting how poor all you Barneses are—just revolting— why doesn't the government cart you all away to some island off Alaska?"

Cliff smiled, aware that she was joking. Still, she sparked his curiosity. "Seriously, though, Sue Ellen," he said, "I know you're not attracted to me for my money . . . was it my devastating good looks that laid you low, or what? You could have had anybody you wanted, you know."

She blushed at the compliment. "I don't really know," she answered, searching for the reason. "I suppose the fact that J.R. hates you so much must have had something to do with it."

"Aha!" Cliff exclaimed, "I suspected as much. If J.R. ever found out you were with me, he would fly through the roof! You picked the relationship you knew would hurt him the most!"

Sue Ellen felt the shock of the truth like a charge of electricity. "That's odd . . . perhaps that's what it was . . . I've gotten so sick of seeing him always get what he wants at other people's expense . . . he's always on the winning side . . . I guess I was tired of putting up with it."

"And so, you came to Cliff Barnes," he said, "a man who has always been a loser . . . who comes from a family that's always lost, particularly at the hands of the Ewings." He nodded in agreement, but there was determination in his tone. "I'll tell you something, Sue Ellen. I have no intention of remaining a loser. There's a difference between losing the battle and losing the war. Do you understand?"

"Of course I do, Cliff," she said, grabbing his arm passionately. "Do you think I could have been so attracted to someone who was really a loser?"

He smiled again, sensing that she was telling him the truth. "Hey," he said, poking her in the ribs playfully, "what do you say we go someplace?"

"By someplace, did you mean your place?" She was looking at him suggestively.

"That is what I had in mind, as a matter of fact," he admitted. "Got the time?"

She nodded, licking her lips.

"If you really have the time," he suggested, "we could get a bite to eat first."

"No thanks," Sue Ellen demurred. "I haven't been feeling well lately. Eating is the last thing I want to do."

Cliff's face clouded over and he took her in his arms. "Sure you're okay?" he asked, worried.

"Why don't be silly," she brushed him off. "Of course I'm all right."

The intercom buzzer sounded on Liz Craig's desk, and she leaned forward to answer it.

"Pam is here to see you," said her secretary.

"Good," said Liz, "show her right in." Clearing off the business that was cluttering her desk, Liz got up and went to the door to greet her favorite employee.

"Hi," Pam said, somewhat tentatively, not knowing why she had been summoned.

"Have a chair, Pam," her boss offered, motioning to one positioned next to the desk.

The both sat down as Pam said, "You called and I came—what's the problem? Have I done something wrong?"

Liz laughed. "Oh, no, it's nothing like that," she insisted. "In fact, rather the opposite. I called you in here to tell you all about your new job. You're being promoted."

Pam's mouth dropped open and she clapped her hands together in delight. "You must be joking!" she cried happily. "We were only discussing this yesterday, and already I get the promotion?"

Liz smiled, shaking her head. "I never joke, Pam. You know me—no sense of humor at all . . . no, I just thought that you should begin moving in more elite circles—the kind you're becoming accustomed to at home."

Pam was confused. Liz was talking in circles, teasing her, leading up to something. "I don't quite understand," she confessed.

"Well," said Liz, "for instance, you'll be needing an up-to-date passport, of course . . ."

Pam nodded, not quite hearing what her boss was saying. "Of course," she repeated. Then it sunk in. "What do you mean, a passport? A passport for what, Liz?"

"Well," said the older woman slowly, "things are quite friendly between our two countries, but as far as I know, the French still require a passport for Americans to enter." Seeing that Pam was still confused, Liz dropped her gift-wrapped bomb-shell. "We—you and I—are going on a trip to a little town called Paris."

"What?" Pam was flabbergasted. Here she was, just a floor-walker, an inventory clerk, and now she would be going to Paris! "But I don't understand, Liz . . . why? I mean, not why, but, well, yes, why? What's the purpose of the trip?"

Liz made a face. "Why, Pam," she said, "I'm surprised at you—what's in Paris besides museums? Fashions, of course. Designs to be bought—and that's where we come in . . . we're buyers—I am, and now you are too."

"Me?" Pam couldn't believe it. Just six weeks before she had gone to New York in her capacity of temporary assistant buyer, and now she was a buyer herself! A real buyer, vested with the power to make decisions for The Store that involved a lot of money. "Why me, Liz?" she needed to know.

"Well," said the older woman, "let me count the ways—you've got a good brain, great taste in fashions, a wonderful sense of style, of what goes with what . . . need I say more? You've got the talent, now it's time you got the on-the-job experience. That's all there is to it."

Pam felt as if she were floating on air. It was all so wonderful! She had expected a promotion, of course, but this . . . this was much more than a promotion—this was a career!

But then, almost before she had had a chance to take it all in, a cloud came over her. Bobby. What was Bobby going to think of all this? It had all been so difficult, just her going to work in the first place! What would he say now that she was going to be on the fast track of career woman? For that matter, what would the rest of the family say when they heard? It was not going to be easy for her to deal with . . . not easy at all.

Liz noticed her hesitation. "Pam . . . you all right? You look like a truck just hit you."

Pam let out a little laugh. "Funny you should put it that way . . . it's all terrific, really it is, but . . . traveling to Paris? I'm not sure how that'll go down at home . . . see, Bobby and I have hammered out an understanding about my working, but it's tenuous, at best, and I don't think trips to Paris come under the umbrella of our agreement."

Liz frowned. Having been a single, working woman for most of her life, she felt very strongly that Pam's career should be her own province, and not her husband's. "I think you should sit down with him and re-negotiate this agreement of yours," she suggested. "Remember, Pam, this kind of opportunity doesn't knock every day . . . it doesn't even usually knock twice."

Pam nodded, knowing that Liz spoke the truth and that she would have to stand up for herself. "That's what I'm going to have to do, I guess," she agreed. "I'm sure he'll understand if I put it properly. I'd better let him know tonight, though, before I lose my resolve." Getting up to go, she turned and thanked Liz once again for the tremendous faith she had shown in her. "How can I ever thank you?" she asked.

"By taking me up on my offer," her boss replied soberly.

Pam nodded. She had every intention of doing so.

Heading for the door she was stopped by a question from Liz. "Hey! When you tell Bobby you're going to Paris, when are you going to tell him you'll be going?"

Pam stopped, realizing that in her inner turmoil she had forgotten to take down the particulars of the proposed trip. "I suppose I should write this all down," she agreed, laughing sheepishly and retracing her steps. "Okay, shoot," she said, taking out a pad and pencil.

Liz looked in her datebook. "Let's see . . ." she said. "Our mission, should you choose to accept it, involves leaving Dallas on the night of the fifteenth. We'll be gone for a week, arriving back in town on the twenty-second. How's that sound to you?"

Pam sat there in a state of shock. The number seventeen loomed before her. Bobby's party! The blue-bloods from back East were coming to Dallas, to the big party she was going to throw for them!

Liz squinted and leaned toward Pam. "Is there something wrong, Pam?"

Pam sighed. "Oh, God, I hope not," she answered. "I really hope not."

Chapter Ten

Attendance at dinner was again sparse, as sparse in numbers, if not in feeling, as that night six weeks earlier when J.R. and Bobby's chairs had stood so awfully empty. J.R.'s chair was vacant, its customary occupant off in Washington on his business trip. Sue Ellen's chair, too, stood empty, as did Lucy's. On the other side sat Pam and Bobby, and Miss Ellie and Jock were in their usual seats.

Surveying the scene, Jock snorted with disgust. "What the hell's goin' on around here these days?" he asked with annoyance. "This family is falling apart at the seams! Where is everybody?"

"Now, Jock," said Miss Ellie. "Don't excite yourself over nothing. I told you at least twice that Lucy is staying overnight at her friend Muriel's. There's nothing wrong with that, so don't act like there is."

"Muriel?" Jock eyed her skeptically, "Muriel who?"

"Muriel Gillis," said Ellie.

"Hmph," he snorted again, cantankerously, "I thought only old ladies were named Muriel anymore. What kind of a name is that for a young girl anyway?" Not being able to prevail on one argument, he had switched tracks to another, but Miss Ellie held fast.

"Muriel Gillis is a nice, quiet girl, and you have no call to go making fun of her name, you crabby old man."

Bobby grinned at her description, imagining the two girls together. "What's a wildcat like Lucy doing with a nice, quiet girl like that?" he teased.

"Now you just hush up, young man," his mother chided him.

"Only kidding." Bobby covered his face with his hands as if warding off an imaginary blow.

Jock lay down his utensils, his steak finished. "All right, so Lucy is accounted for. I know where J.R. is, and I know what he's doin', but he's been away an awful lot lately, a lot more than is decent, if you ask me. That's J.R. Now what about Sue Ellen. You haven't 'told me a million times' where *she* is, Ellie."

Miss Ellie lowered her head patiently, drawing on her enormous reserves of forbearance, and then replied softly, "No, I didn't, Jock. As it happens, Sue Ellen called just before dinner to say that she'd bumped into some old acquaintances in town and that she was going to go out to dinner and spend the evening with them. She said she'd be back around eleven, and not to wait up for her. Is that a complete enough accounting for you, Mr. Nosybody Ewing?"

Jock shook his head, refusing as he always did to

admit defeat, and retreat graciously. "I don't understand how young people behave these days. I read in the papers that this is the 'me' generation, and I guess it is all right, because everybody seems to be takin' off in his or her own direction, regardless of everybody else. There's no real sense of family anymore . . . I can't remember more than once in the last month when we all sat down to dinner together as a family. I guess the times have passed me by or something . . ." His voice faded into a low grumble of protest.

Bobby intervened, sensing that his mother's patience was spent. "Look, Daddy, there may be some truth in what you say, but I don't believe it's all that bad. After all, Lucy is really a grown-up now, and it's only right that she start getting out on her own. Why, next year she'll be at college. And as for the rest of us, the truth is that there's a lot of business matters we all have to attend to."

Pam lay down her fork and knife and stared at her plate, the mouthful she had swallowed sticking in her throat. She knew that if all went as planned, there would soon be another empty seat at the table—her own. Realizing that soon she would have to tell her husband the news filled her with dread and panic.

"Well, there's no need to beat up on me." Jock was frowning. "Two against one's not fair, and therefore I give up." Pushing his chair back from the table, he said, "Now you've all gone and spoiled my appetite. I don't believe I'll have any dessert tonight. I'm gonna get me some fresh air . . . pretty night out there, under the stars. Miss Ellie? Care to join me for a little walk around the spread?"

Miss Ellie smiled at him warmly. What a nice way to end an argument. That was one of the things she loved best about her husband: suddenly, without warning, he was able to express his warmth, his vulnerability. It was what set him apart, to her, from all the other roughneck cowboys she had known. "I'd love to, Jock," she took his hand. "Would you two like to join us?" She turned to Pam and Bobby.

Pam declined, saying she wanted some coffee. In the first place, it was obvious that neither Jock nor Ellie really wanted them along, looking forward as they were to a little intimacy of their own; and in the second place, now was as good a time as any to broach the big subject of the moment.

Jock and Ellie left, and Teresa came and went after pouring Pam's coffee.

Bobby didn't want any. Somehow, he sensed that something was up. "You didn't say a word all during dinner," he remarked.

It was true, she reflected, biting her lip. She wasn't very good at hiding her feelings, and she knew it.

"It isn't because you had nothing to say, is it?" he asked her.

She shook her head.

"Well, what's been on your mind, then? Want to talk about it?"

"Yes, I do, Bobby," she admitted. Watching as Raoul cleared the table, she suddenly felt tremendously uncomfortable. "Would you mind," she asked him, "if we go into the living room to talk about this?"

Bobby shrugged. It was all the same to him. But her discomfort suggested to him that it was a matter of great importance to both of them; it didn't appear as though this was going to be an easy conversation.

Taking her coffee with her, she led him through the entryway into the other room. Neither of them said a word as Pam seated herself on a sofa and Bobby went to the bar and poured himself a brandy.

He was beginning to feel nervous. "All right, let's hear it," he said, gesturing for her to begin.

"Uhh . . ." she stammered, looking for the words. "It has to do with the party . . ." She suddenly went silent from fear.

"What about the party," Bobby prodded her, to get her going again. "Did you take my advice and see Sue Ellen about it?"

"I met her at lunchtime, but she wasn't all that helpful. She just gave me the name of her caterer, and said he'd handle all the details. She seemed annoyed that I had asked for her time, but she did give me that number anyway."

Bobby slapped his knees, satisfied that he had understood the problem. "There, you see?" he assured her. "I told you there would be no problem throwing this party."

Faced with his intractable optimism, she could not do it. She could not tackle the problem directly. And so she began to equivocate, offering roundabout hints to probe his feelings, to see whether he would understand about the trip to Paris. "Yes, but see, Bobby, I'm not ready . . . there's no way I can be ready by the seventeenth . . . it's so soon! Less than two weeks . . . why, I don't even have a decent dress to wear . . . all my party dresses are out of style, and there are a million other things to do . . ."

Bobby put his arm around her shoulder and drew her to him. "Look, Pammy," he counseled her, "you're being hysterical about this. You work in a high-fashion shop, and I'm sure you can pick out something suitable. And you know you can afford it—you might even get something off for being an employee!"

Pam pressed her point, still unable to bring up the promotion or the trip. "Please, Bobby, let's postpone the party—just for a week or so . . . that would make a world of difference, really it would! You don't know how much I'd appreciate it . . ."

Bobby brushed her hair out of her face tenderly and kissed her lightly on the lips. "Pamela, the seventeenth was not my idea . . . the people from back East are coming then, and that's when it has to be. This is the first time they've ever been out here, and if we don't throw the party for them, who knows when or whether we'll have the chance again? Now is the time . . . these guys want to build right now, and they're willing to be sold. We've got to strike when the iron is hot."

Pam bowed her head, defeated. "This is it then?" she asked dolefully. "It's life or death for you?"

"For you and me both," he said. "Like I told you, their opinion of you is gonna be just as important as what they think of me."

Pam took a deep breath. Her love for her husband and her need for a career of her own had run smack dab into each other. One of them was going to have to give way, and Pam did not hesitate to choose. "All right, Bobby. The seventeenth it'll be."

She had done it. She felt a great wave of grief come over her for the opportunity she had allowed to die. She wondered if she had done the right thing, but she knew at the same time that she had done what she had to do.

Seeing how downcast she was, Bobby shook his head in wonderment. "Hey," he said, "it's not that bad, honey . . . it'll be a great party, believe me . . . and what if it isn't? We'll survive . . . it's just a party, after all."

Pam looked at him in agony. How ironic that he was trying to cheer her up with the very words that were tearing her apart. "It's only a party . . . it's only a party . . ." It was only a party, but it was so much more . . . so much more . . .

As badly as she had felt on and off during the last few days, the knot in Sue Ellen's stomach grew tighter than ever as she sat in the plush waiting room of the doctor's office. Somewhere above her head there was a hidden speaker playing Muzak softly. The music, meant to be soothing, had the opposite effect as every muscle and nerve in her body screamed with anxiety. It was as if the notes of one song were rubbing against the notes of another. The dissonance grated on her nerves until she could hardly stand it, and she almost got up to leave. But at that moment the nurse appeared and asked her to follow.

Something was wrong with her and she knew it. For days now, she had kept telling herself that it was the strain, the tension of having an illicit affair for the very first time. But the feeling had grown worse and worse, and now she knew that whatever the initial causes, there was now something physically wrong with her, and she dreaded coming to the doctor. Nevertheless, she had made the appointment, feeling that certainty was better than this vague state of not knowing, of imagining all the worst possible outcomes. At least now, however bad the news was, she would know something for sure.

The nurse left her to herself in the white—too white—examination room, where there was no Muzak, at least. She looked around her at the implements of healing, but they reminded her of nothing but sickness. She, who had never been sick a day in her life! Was she now about to go to the hospital? Or have an operation? Or worse? Sue Ellen's thoughts began to run away with her completely. Throughout the past days, her romance with Cliff had taken her mind off the queasiness, the faint feelings, the dizziness and weakness. But now, alone in the world of medicine, the fear closed in on her, and she felt completely alone and helpless. Why didn't the doctor come?

Finally, Dr. Jason White entered, startling Sue Ellen so that she gasped in shock. Her nerves were definitely on edge, and the doctor, an observant man, noted her discomfiture. He was a white-haired, distinguished man in his mid-fifties, and he wore a white medical jacket over his shirt and tie. Smiling, he began his examination.

When he had finished, she asked him timidly, "Any idea what's wrong with me, doctor?" She braced herself for his reply.

"I don't hazard guesses, Mrs. Ewing," he said. "I will say this, though—I don't think it's anything too serious."

Sue Ellen felt only an instant of relief, which was broken by a wave of faintness. "But doctor," she protested, "if it's nothing serious, why do I feel so terrible?"

The doctor shrugged. "I'm only human, Mrs. Ewing," he reminded her. "The tests will tell us more. In the meantime, it could be hundreds of things, as far as I can tell. I'm sorry. I know doctors are supposed to know everything, but we only know what we can see, and what tests tell us."

She smiled back at him, understanding. "As soon as you know . . ." she prompted him.

"As soon as I know," he finished her sentence for her, "you'll know too. The tests should be back sometime later today. I'll call you." She rose and shook his hand, turning to go. "Oh, while I've got you here—" he stopped her. "Your husband is long overdue for a checkup. I wish you'd tell him to get on down here as soon as he can."

She nodded. "I'll do that, doctor . . . as soon as I see him."

She wondered when that would be.

Cliff Barnes' office was small and crowded in the best of times, but now, in the wake of his recent election defeat, it was a disaster area. Boxes of buttons lay piled in the corners along with hundreds of bumper stickers, and posters were stacked everywhere. Cliff had thought about throwing all of it away, but had had second thoughts. After all, he thought he might someday run again, and they would come in handy in that case. Why spend good campaign money on new materials when you could just as easily use the old ones?

One of the posters was tacked on the wall behind his desk, a huge likeness of his face staring down over his shoulder all day long. On the poster, under the headline "Barnes for State Senate," were scrawled the words "Better luck next time . . . try, try again."

Cliff was an indefatigable doodler, and even now, as he sat at his desk talking to his sister Pam, he held across his lap another poster on which he was doing yet another doodle. His feet were up on the desk to prop the poster up in his lap, and he scribbled away with a big, black magic marker.

There was an edge of bitterness in his voice. "You know, Pam, just give them enough time. Sooner or later, the Ewings will have every penny of wealth in this state. It's inevitable." He was referring to the big deal Bobby was working on. Pam had come to him for advice, and he was giving it to her with both barrels.

"Come on, Cliff, be serious," she pleaded. "Bobby really wants this deal, and I don't want to be the one who screws it up for him."

Her brother looked at her skeptically. "If it means as much to him as you say it does, and he means as much to you as you say he does, then why are you here asking me for advice?"

Pam sighed heavily. "Because there are other factors. My job is just as important to me as Bobby's deal is to him. It's not an easy choice, but—"

He interrupted her. "Aha! *But*! It always comes down to *but*, doesn't it? Your job is important, *but* Bobby disapproves. Bobby's a great guy, *but* he's a Ewing. He's so understanding, *but* will he understand about this trip to Paris? I've got a *but* for you, Pam—this deal's important to Bobby, granted, *but* is it really all that important for you to be there?"

Pam squirmed in her chair, running it all over in her mind. "I know I have as much right to be successful as Bobby does, but—" she stopped herself, realizing what she had said. "It really is the magic word, isn't it?" she said, wonderingly.

He smiled back at her, secretly pleased that her marriage to the Ewing family had caused so many problems for her. He wasn't going to say "I told you so," but he was going to let her know he was thinking it.

"Look, sis," he said finally, in his most lawyerly fashion, laying out the case as he would before a jury, "it's like this—there's no way I can really be of any help to you on this one. I'm sorry to have to say it, but it's the truth and nothing but the truth. You told me on the phone that you wanted to discuss it with me, and so we've discussed it. Okay. The truth is, though, that on a question like this a person is really on his or her own in the final analysis. And no matter what advice I gave you, you'd go and do whatever you thought was right anyway. *But*—that old magic word—*but*, let me lay out the problem and the possible solutions as I see them." He pointed his magic marker in the air for emphasis.

"Go ahead," Pam urged him.

"It's like this—you can either go on this trip with your boss and take the heavy artillery you're sure to get from Bobby and the Ewings, or you can pass the opportunity by for the sake of marital bliss, in which case you'll always wonder what you might have accomplished in your career if you'd have gone ahead with it. The problems with the first option are self-evident. The problems with the second are, A—will you always resent your husband and his family for standing in the way of your career? And B—your brother thinks you should tell them all to go to hell, and you should set sail for gay *Paree*! That's about the size of it, as I see it." He fell silent, waiting for her comment.

"So," she said, nodding sagely and sadly. "So that's what it comes down to in the end—tell the Ewings to go to hell. That seems to be all you ever have to say about them. You hate them so much that you can only see things in black and white where they're concerned."

He raised his eyebrows playfully. "You're not being fair to me, Pamela. I'm not always against the Ewings . . . why in fact, there's one Ewing I'm very much in favor of!" He could not repress a smile as he watched his deliberate double entendre take effect.

Pam, of course, having no inkling of what was going on between Cliff and Sue Ellen, thought he meant *her*. Smiling, she leaned forward and patted him on the arm. "Cliff, that's sweet of you. I'm in favor of you, too . . . really I am." Getting up to go, she leaned over to kiss him on the cheek. He hid the doodle he was drawing from her view as he submitted his cheek to her kiss.

"See you soon, okay?" she said.

"Right, sis—and give me a call to let me know what you decide, will you?"

Pam laughed derisively. "Yeah," she said, "if I ever do decide one way or the other . . ."

She was gone, closing the door behind her. When her footsteps were safely out of earshot, Cliff held up the poster in front of him to survey the results of his artwork. There, on his larger-than-life black-and-white face, were drawn a heavy black moustache and goatee, and a pair of horns to match.

Liz Craig stood by an easel that had been set up in her office. Poised on it were several sketches drawn by free-lance designers who stood, tense and waiting, while Liz surveyed their designs and rendered her judgments. "That's very nice, Kenny," she said, patting one of them gently on the back and tousling his hair flirtatiously. "You have a real flair for the outrageous . . . keep it up." Taking the approved sketch off the easel, she had begun to consider the next design when her intercom buzzer sounded. "What is it, Sheila?" she asked her secretary.

"Mr. Bobby Ewing is here to see you, Ms. Craig. He's in the couturier shop, and he told me to ask you if you would meet him there."

Liz raised herself to an upright position and considered this surprise visit. What did Bobby Ewing possibly want to talk with her about? Reflecting for a moment, she decided that it could only be about Pam's promotion, and that if he had come to the store in person to discuss it, he must not be very happy about it. Sure that she had a tough argument ahead of her, she braced herself. "Tell him I'll be out in a moment," she told Sheila. Apologizing to her disappointed designers for the interruption, she straightened her dress and walked out the door onto the sales floor.

In the couturier's shop, Bobby stood surveying the mannequins and the salesladies. The couturier's shop was, as its name suggested, the most expensive area in The Store, and all the salesladies—even the mannequins—wore snobbish expressions on their faces. Bobby stood there looking slightly baffled in the unaccustomed surroundings. He was used to luxury, to be sure, but not, perhaps, to high fashion. He stood gazing in particular at one very tall model, perhaps all of six feet, wearing a filmy yet severe dress on her ultra-slender figure. It was all so bizarre, he was thinking. All these expensive clothes seemed to be made to adorn figures that almost no women possessed. He wondered how Pam, with her ample, womanly curves, would look in such a dress. Ridiculous, he decided. He hoped that she wouldn't ever get it into her head to wear one home!

Liz walked up behind him unnoticed. "Ahem," she said, amused by his evident awkwardness. "Do you see anything you'd like to try on, Bobby? I'm not sure there's anything that will fit you, but we do free alterations . . ."

Bobby laughed, disarmed, as Liz had intended. "I don't think there's anything to fit me, or anybody else, for that matter . . . who buys these things, anyway, if you don't mind my asking?"

Liz smiled, not offended, knowing as she did that he was right in his observations. "Many of our customers are matronly women, about five-foot-three and tending to fat," she explained. "They all seem to think these dresses fit them just right. Don't ask me why, but of course I don't try very hard to talk them out of buying . . ." She stopped joking, aware again that he had come with a purpose. "What can I do for you, Bobby? You didn't come to buy a dress, did you?"

"As a matter of fact, Liz, that's exactly why I came."

Liz's mouth hung open. It was the last thing she had expected him to say.

"I want to buy Pam a dress, and I have no idea which one would be good for her. It has to be perfect, you see, and I thought . . . well, that you could give me some help in picking it out."

Liz could hardly believe her ears! What a man Bobby was—handsome and bright as anything, a man's man, to be sure, yet sensitive enough to understand his wife's need for her own career, and supportive enough to come to The Store himself to pick out her dress for Paris! "Is there some special reason you want to buy her a dress, Bobby?" she asked, innocently. "What sort of thing did you have in mind?"

"Well, let's put it this way," he said with a wink, "I want it to be something that'll make a great first impression . . . I want her to look her very best. There's something real important coming up in her life."

Liz laughed. "I know all about it, Bobby—and I think you're very sweet."

Bobby was puzzled. "She told you about it? Well, sure, I guess she would . . ."

Liz ignored his confusion and continued confidentially, "She said she was going to break it to you last night. I'm glad you took it so well. That kind of sensitivity is so rare in men." She patted him on the shoulder affectionately.

Suddenly Bobby felt ill at ease. He was beginning to get the distinct impression that Liz was talking about something other than the big party, something entirely different, something he knew nothing about. He was determined to find out what it was without Liz knowing he suspected anything. He did not want to put her on her guard now that she was being so open with him.

"Why shouldn't I take it well?" he inquired, hoping she would divulge some more information.

"Well," said Liz, as if it were obvious, "there are a lot of husbands around who wouldn't take kindly to their wives traveling to Paris without them—and at a moment's notice, to boot! I think it's really big of you, Bobby, and you deserve a lot of credit."

"Paris . . ." The word escaped his lips before he could stop it. So that was it! That was what all the probing questions of the night before had been about! Why hadn't she told him? Was there more? "Uh, yes, of course . . ." he tried to cover his surprise. "Um, Liz, she told me when she was leaving, but I forgot . . . so many things on my mind . . . when was it again?"

"We leave on the fifteenth and come back on the twenty-second," she offered. "I know I've said this already, but I just have to compliment you again. All my life I've been looking for a man who was as understanding as you are. Pam's a lucky woman. And you won't be sorry, Bobby, really you won't—this is a really big break for her, career-wise—she'll be meeting a lot of big buyers and designers. It's the biggest fashion show of the season, and she'll be making a lot of important decisions. With her taste, she'll be a smash, you'll see. There's no telling how far she can go in this business."

"Uh . . . yeah . . . I guess so . . ." Bobby was as close to speechless as a person can get. He had to get out of there and talk to Pam right away, to see how much this really meant to her, what it meant for them. Suddenly his life was in crisis; he felt his breath catch in his throat. "Uh, listen, Liz . . . that dress we were talking about . . ."

"Oh!" she cooed happily. "Let me show you this wonderful little number we've got upstairs! It's very expensive, but I know once you see it, you're going to want it for Pam—she'll be the star of the show in this dress, I can promise you that." And, without waiting for a reply, she turned and started up the stairs. An agonized Bobby trudged obediently after her, his brows furrowed in worry, and his mind in silent turmoil.

Raoul opened the screen door with his back, and, holding the large tray with iced tea in both his hands, walked onto the patio where the family was gathered around the pool under their umbrellas in the heat of the afternoon. Sue Ellen sat silently, her mind on her health, and on Cliff. It was all she could do to make an occasional contribution to the poolside conversation. For his part, Bobby could not even manage that much. Pamela had still not returned from her luncheon with Cliff, and his eyes focused on the front gate where he waited for her car to materialize, his fingers drumming the table impatiently. Raoul left his drink beside him, but Bobby didn't even notice that it was there.

The conversation was being carried on among the other three poolside sunbathers—Lucy, Jock and Ellie. Lucy was complaining, as usual, about not having a car of her own. "When I was over at Muriel Gillis' the other night," she was saying, "her father drove home in her second car! That's

DALLAS

right—her *second* car! We've got ten times as much money as the Gillis', and not only don't I have a car of my own, but I don't even get to drive anybody else's car! Now, I ask you, is that fair?"

Miss Ellie smiled, her patience endless. "Lucy, haven't we discussed this before, dear? It seems to me the issue is closed. It's not going to help to complain about it."

Lucy stamped her feet on the cement in frustration. "But I want a car of my own!" she cried shrilly. "I keep saying the same thing over and over again, because nobody ever listens to what I'm saying! It's like I live with a bunch of deaf people! Why doesn't anybody in this family care about what I want?"

It was Jock's turn to say something. "Lucy," he droned, "I don't understand why you're in such a big rush to have a car. Anytime you ever want to go anywhere, somebody's here to drive you. It's not everybody who has their own personal chauffeur." He meant Sue Ellen, who normally would have been miffed at being described as a chauffeur, but who was too preoccupied to care at the moment.

"Has it occurred to you, Granddaddy, that I might want to go someplace alone once in a while?" She was well aware that it had occurred to him, and to everyone else, and she was also aware that, more than any other reason, that was why they refused to buy her a car of her own. They did not want her going off alone and getting into trouble. As far as they were concerned, she had managed to get into enough trouble without the benefit of a car to assist her.

Sue Ellen admitted as much when she looked up and said, "We feel it's in your best interests that you be accompanied when you want to go someplace, Lucy dear."

Lucy felt like spitting. "You don't feel at all, Sue Ellen," she said bitterly, "that's your problem."

Miss Ellie sat up, knowing it was time to head off the argument. "Let's put this on the shelf for another time, shall we?"

But Lucy wasn't yet ready to throw in the towel, worked up as she had become over the issue. She turned to Bobby for his opinion. "Uncle Bobby," she nudged him, "you understand, don't you? Tell them it's not fair!"

Bobby shook his head, rudely awakened from his reverie. "Huh?" he said, dazed.

"About me not having a car!" she repeated impatiently. "Tell them I should have one!"

"Well, Lucy," he said apologetically, "I don't know that I should get involved in this one . . . it looks to be a pretty hot topic, and I haven't given it any thought one way or the other."

Instead of being defeated by his refusal to back her up, Lucy was exultant. "I want you all to notice that at least Uncle Bobby is being honest. He hasn't given it any thought, and he admits it. I think you all ought to admit the same thing, because there's not a one of you here who's even considered it!"

Fortunately for all of them, Pam picked that moment to drive up. Bobby sprang up and ran over to her. "Hi, sweetheart," she said gaily as she emerged from the car. Kissing him on the cheek, she put her arm around his waist and they walked back to the patio together. The all-around greetings were interrupted by the ringing of the poolside phone, and Lucy went over to answer it.

"Yes?" she said. "Oh, yes, she is . . . just hold on a minute, will you?" She turned back to the family. "It's some doctor . . . for you, Sue Ellen," she said, a note of curiosity in her voice.

Sue Ellen took the phone from her, and dragged the wire as far away from the others as it would go. Of course, far as she could manage to get, she was still well within earshot. What a fool she had been, she thought to herself, not to have been alone in the house waiting for the call. Then again, if she was going to die, they were all going to know sooner or later anyway.

"This is Mrs. Ewing. Hello Doctor," she whispered. Then she was silent for a long moment as she received the news. Her face turned gray as she listened, a fact that was not lost on the family, who were becoming more curious with every moment. "What? Oh, no, Doctor, you must be mistaken . . . it can't be! . . . I . . . I see . . . yes, thank you, doctor . . . yes, of course. I understand. I'll see you then." She slowly hung up the phone, staring at it all the while in shock.

Seeing that Sue Ellen was standing there, not moving at all, Miss Ellie went to her side. "What is it, dear? What did the doctor say? Is there something wrong?"

Sue Ellen shook her head. "No, there's nothing wrong, Miss Ellie," she said dully, still in a daze.

"Well, then what did the doctor say?"

Sue Ellen turned to face her mother-in-law, to face them all, ten eyes staring at her. "The doctor?" she repeated through her fog. "He just said that I'm pregnant."

Chapter Eleven

There was a long moment of silence while the news sank in. Like Sue Ellen, they were all somewhat dazed. Then, suddenly, as if a dam had broken, they all came rushing forward to embrace her. Sue Ellen, by contrast, remained stupefied, as if she still could not comprehend the fact that she was going to have a child, after all the years of trying in vain, and then not even trying anymore. It was all too much for her to take in at once. She just stood there as they congratulated her, their faces beaming.

"Well, what do you know about that!" roared Jock ecstatically. "Pregnant! After all these years! I can't believe it's true! I don't mind tellin' you, girl, I'd about given up on you! Ha, ha!" He hugged her warmly.

"Oh, Sue Ellen, I'm so happy!" said Miss Ellie, beaming.

The prospect of more grandchildren, the next Ewing generation, had been paramount in the parents' minds for years, and the news was the best they could have heard.

Lucy, too, was happy, as much as she couldn't stand Sue Ellen. How could she not be happy? Finally, she would not be the baby around Southfork! "Sue Ellen, that's great! Really great!"

Bobby, for his part, was happy for Sue Ellen, to be sure, but he was also troubled. He was watching his own wife, searching her face to see how she felt about the news. Her own brief pregnancy the year before had ended in a tragic miscarriage, and now, with her career in full bloom, it was not likely they would have children for some time to come. How did Pam feel about what had happened? Her smiling face gave no sign of distress, but Bobby wondered nonetheless. Approaching Sue Ellen, he kissed her on the cheek and took her hand in his. "It's wonderful, Sue Ellen. I know you've been waiting a long time, and I wish you the best, I really do."

For the first time, Sue Ellen was able to respond. She thanked him for his kind words and turned to Pam who now approached her.

"Oh, Sue Ellen," she beamed, "you're going to have a baby! I'm so delighted! You've always wanted it, and now it's coming true!"

There were tears in Pam's eyes, and in Sue Ellen's, too. As much as they had hated each other at times, they were united now in the joy of the moment, and there was real love between them.

"I believe you really are sincere about that, Pamela. Thank you so much. That's very generous of you."

The two women embraced, hugging each other tightly. All the others looked on silently, appreciating what a big moment it was for both of them, for the whole family, in fact. Jock and Ellie were particularly gratified to see their two daughters-in-law embrace. It signified to them a future of family harmony and peace, and it made them very happy.

When the embrace finally ended, Bobby had a thought. "Hey, everybody," he said. "I don't know about you all, but I have a feeling J.R. might be interested in hearing about this! What do you say we give him a call in Washington, Daddy?"

Jock roared with laughter, as happy as he had been in his life. "You know, with all the excitement, I almost forgot about that boy! Hand me that phone, would you? I only hope I can remember the damn number where he's stayin'!" And he laughed again as he dialed the number, which, of course, he knew perfectly well. Everyone gathered 'round Jock as he held the bright yellow receiver in his hand and listened to the phone ring 1,500 miles away.

J.R. Ewing's suite was alive with people. There was a party in full swing, and J.R. stood in the middle of it all surveying what he had wrought, a big smile on his face and his arm around Judy. All around the room congressmen, judges and lobbyists chased after lovely young ladies. Acquaintances were made, phone numbers exchanged, secrets whispered, contracts sealed. J.R. was spreading the "three B's" around, and they were doing their work. He almost didn't hear the phone ringing all the way over on the other side of the suite.

Excusing himself to Judy, he headed across the room waving to the happy party-goers as he went.

"Hello," he said into the phone. On the other end he could barely hear his father over the noise in the room.

"J.R.? What the hell's goin' on up there?"

"Just a little party for the boys on the hill, Daddy." J.R. smiled. "What's up back home? Everything all right?"

Apparently Jock was having trouble hearing him, for he ignored J.R.'s question and instead shouted into the phone, "Hold on, boy. I'm gonna put Sue Ellen on . . . she's got something she wants to say to you."

There was a fumbling on the line as J.R. waited, his brows furrowed. What could that woman possibly want? Why was she bothering him while he was on an important business trip? She was a royal pain, he decided. Looking across the room at Judy, he mentally compared the two women and found Sue Ellen greatly wanting. So much of the thrill of a woman, he reflected, lay in the chase . . .

"J.R.? That you?" She sounded nervous, as well she should.

"You got a lot of nerve, Sue Ellen, calling me here. Do you realize I'm in the middle of entertaining a dozen congressmen and senators here? What do you think you're doin'?"

There was a slight pause before she replied, "Um . . . there was . . . there was something I thought I ought to tell you . . . I thought you might want to know about this right away, darlin'."

J.R. shuffled his feet impatiently. Looking across the room, he noticed one of the lobbyists engaged in close conversation with Judy, his arm around her affectionately. A pang of jealousy and desire passed through J.R. as he watched, tied to the phone.

"Well, let's hear it then, but make it fast, will you. I'm busy."

What Sue Ellen said next gave him the shock of his life. "All right, here it is. We're gonna have a baby, J.R. . . . you and me . . . I'm pregnant."

J.R. felt his legs about to buckle as his breath caught in his throat. The room was spinning all around him, but he remained stock still, the phone lowered momentarily from his ear to his side as he stood there, rooted to the spot. "Pregnant!" he managed to say after a moment raising the phone back to his mouth. "Pregnant? What do you mean, pregnant? Are you kidding?" And then, as he realized she wasn't kidding, he muttered, "Pregnant . . . my goodness . . . my goodness . . ."

Sue Ellen could not tell at all from his tone of voice how he felt about the news, other than the fact that he was obviously surprised. When he fell silent, she asked him if he was still there. She wished she could have been a fly on the wall in Washington to see his initial reaction.

He finally recovered sufficiently to say, "Why, isn't that wonderful! What do you know . . . a baby!" He barely knew what he was saying or why he was saying it.

"J.R." asked Sue Ellen, trying to sound as sweet as possible, not only for his sake, but for the sake of the family crowded around her straining to hear J.R.'s reaction, "how do you feel, darling? Are you happy?"

"Well, my, my, my . . ." J.R. rambled on. "Of course I'm happy, what do you mean by that? I'm truly happy, Sue Ellen." He was speaking too loudly now, drawing the attention of some of the nearby party guests. They had no idea what he was

talking about and didn't really care, but the volume
of his remarks told them that he was drunk,
which he was, but only a little. "Listen, here, Sue
Ellen—" Looking around him, he saw the glances
of his guests and knew he had to get off the phone
right away and get himself together, at least till he
was alone and could sort things out. His whole life
was changed, and he needed to think about the
implications of all this. "Listen here, Sue Ellen,"
he said again, trying to eliminate the sound of
discomfort from his voice, "I've got to hang up
now . . . I'm in the middle of a party, and I can't
talk to you . . . I'll come home tomorrow, on the
first flight to Dallas." He heard only silence on the
other end, and assumed she was waiting to hear
more. "Uh, see, it's too late to catch a plane
tonight, otherwise I'd be on one, believe me. I'll
see you in the morning, y'hear?"

There was a long moment before she answered
him. "I hear you, J.R." And then, "I love you,
darlin'."

She waited, expecting to hear him say "I love
you too," but she was disappointed. Even at a
moment such as this, the most affection he could
muster was, "Take good care of yourself, Sue
Ellen. Don't strain yourself or anything. I'll see you
tomorrow."

She was about to hang up when she heard him
shout into the phone for her not to.

"Oh! By the way—what did Daddy say about
it?" Stunned as he was, apparently J.R. was able to
think as far as his father's reaction, crucial as it was
to his position in the family and the business.

"He's ecstatic, of course," she replied, not a
little irritated at his lack of affection for her. "Why

wouldn't he be? Everybody's just thrilled. I'll see you tomorrow, then. I'll—'' She stopped short. He had hung up as soon as she'd told him that Jock was happy. How typical of him, she thought, as she hung up the phone.

J.R. looked over at Judy still flirting with the lobbyist at the other end of the room. Then he turned away from that little scene, and looked himself up and down in the nearby mirror, scrutinizing himself carefully. A baby, he thought to himself . . . a little J.R. . . . somebody to take over for him when he was gone . . . somebody to give all the power and money to someday . . . someone to teach the techniques of success to . . . someone to guide and protect . . . a baby all his own, to mold and shape in his own image.

He began to smile at himself, and the smile grew bigger and bigger, finally breaking out into a great big laugh which rocked the room and drew the attention of all its occupants. But he did not tell them that he was about to become a father. He did not want to spread it around just yet. He merely stood there laughing uproariously—J.R. Ewing, the man of mystery and power.

In the dark of the country night, the few lights remaining on at Southfork Ranch shone like beacons. In the kitchen, Raoul and Teresa were just finishing up for the night. In the entryway, the light was on awaiting Sue Ellen's return. She had gone out to see her old friend again.

Bobby and Pam lay sprawled on their bed in the dark room, lit only by the strong shafts of moonlight pouring through the white lace curtains. They were both wide awake and staring at the ceiling, their minds full of conflicting thoughts, full of anxieties. Bobby couldn't concentrate; what with babies, trips to Paris, jobs—his mind flitted from one thought to another helplessly, unable to focus on any one thing for more than a few minutes, unable to make any sense out of the situation. He felt he could not bring up the trip seeing that she had not seen fit to tell him about it. Why didn't she tell him? He waited silently, hoping that she would say something of her own accord.

It was Pam who finally broke the silence thick as a fog in the room, but she spoke about something else. "You awake?" she asked him, sounding very tentative, perhaps wishing that he was asleep so that she wouldn't have to say anything.

"I'm awake," he answered.

"Bobby, I'm so sorry . . ." her voice trailed off.

He could not tell whether she was crying or not, but there was certainly deep sadness and regret in her voice. "What is it you're sorry for, Pammy?" he asked her gently, hoping to give her the opportunity to tell him about Paris.

"When Sue Ellen made her announcement, I saw your face," she said. "There was pain in it . . . so much pain. I know how much you wanted me to get pregnant right away, Bobby. I know what it would have meant to you. I'm sorry it wasn't me."

He turned to her lovingly. She must have been thinking about the miscarriage, he realized. She would have had a baby by now, and there would have been no job, no trip to Paris, no threat to their relationship. "It doesn't matter about Sue Ellen being the first," he assured her, "not to me, anyway. Not that it wouldn't have been a good thing, but . . . there are more important things.

Besides, if you think about it, it means a lot more to Sue Ellen and J.R. than it would have to us. They're so jumpy about their place in the family hierarchy . . . and they've tried for so long . . .''

Pam was silent. She knew it was true. Seven years of trying. It must have been hell for Sue Ellen. No wonder she had been so catty when Pam had been pregnant. She felt truly glad that Sue Ellen would now be having a baby. "Yes . . . maybe Sue Ellen will be a little nicer to be around now," she reflected.

"J.R. too!" Bobby pointed out. "Just think—now that he knows he's going to be a father, he won't be so keyed up to beat me out all the time, and we won't have to be constantly wrestling for supremacy. It just might mellow him out enough for us to be brotherly again. It sure would be relaxing not to have to watch out for him all the time, not to have to be his opponent on every little thing . . .''

Pam smiled wistfully at the ceiling upon which she had painted, in her mind's eye, a larger-than-life version of Bobby's face. How sweet he was. Marriage had been such an impulsive thing to do at the time, but now, after more than a year, she could see clearly that her instincts about him had been right—he was a good and decent man, and he loved her as well as he could love her, which was very well indeed. How wonderful and kind of him to forgive his brother all the wrongs done him, to wish him well, and to hope for a better relationship. He was a Ewing in many ways . . . but in all the good ways. He had even learned to live with her going to work instead of having a child.

"Wouldn't it be funny," she posited, "if my

going to work wound up being a good thing for all of us?"

He laughed, nodding in agreement. "It might work out pretty well at that," he admitted.

Now. Now was the moment. The door was open to discussion, there was trust and intimacy and harmony between them. She would tell him now, or she never would. "Sweetheart," he said, moving to her and taking her face in his hands tenderly. He kissed her, a kiss with a message behind it—*Trust me . . . tell me . . . I love you with all my heart . . . I want the best for you*. Out loud he said, "That job really does make you happy, huh? You haven't come to feel differently about it?"

"Oh, it's . . . it's wonderful for me, really . . . it gives me a sense of myself, on my own . . . who I am without my husband or my family to define me. And I feel like I'm really accomplishing something relevant, too. I get to feel like I'm capable, and a grown-up." Seeing that he was happy for her, but also sad to hear it, she added, "Oh—I don't mean to keep at it for the rest of my life, mind you—all I'm saying is that it's the most wonderful thing in my life right now—except for you, of course."

She was teasing him with this last, but Bobby did not react as if he had gotten the joke, or even heard her words at all. He was staring at her, waiting for her to tell him, waiting for her to say those magic words which would make them whole again. Finally, seeing that she was not going to tell him after all, Bobby relaxed his gaze. "If it works for you, Pam, I'm for it. I'm behind you one hundred percent."

He meant it, too. But he was also troubled. Evidently she could not trust him even under the best of circumstances. He felt that her job was driving them ever farther apart. Nevertheless, he was determined to lend her his support, even if it cost them their marriage. It was the right thing to do, and he was going to do it, no matter what.

As for Pam, she, too, felt a letdown. She could not bear to tell him, and so she didn't. Seeing how much he was behind her, how much he was willing to be flexible to suit her needs, made it impossible to disappoint him like that. She had to make a decision, to do something, and fast . . . but what could she do?

It had been a night of passionate love-making. Sue Ellen had given herself with a relentless abandon and an insatiable energy born of the still unacknowledged fact that this was the last time. Cliff sensed that there was a difference in her, but he didn't know why. He happily gave himself up to it, not bothering too much with what might lie behind such a consuming passion. Afterwards, she begged him to hold her tightly, and they fell asleep without speaking, close as two people can lie to each other, and yet so far apart.

In the morning Cliff made breakfast, but Sue Ellen wasn't up to having any. She asked instead that he drive her to the park at Bachman Lake for a walk—that lake where they had spent those precious hours falling in love. He drove her there, sensing strongly now that there was something on her mind, something she wanted to talk to him about, something difficult for her to say.

They walked silently for a while beneath the spreading shade trees along the lake until they came to the bed of flowers from which Cliff had once picked her a bouquet. Sue Ellen stopped and looked down at it fondly. He knew that she was about to broach a difficult subject, and he waited for her to work up her courage.

Finally she spoke, without raising her head to look at him. "Cliff, when you think about me, what do you feel?"

It was a strange way to begin. "Isn't it a little early in the day to be discussing our gut feelings?" He didn't say it to be difficult; he sensed that something was up, and he wanted to hold his feelings in reserve.

"Please tell me, Cliff—how do you feel about me—in your heart?"

Was she asking him to declare that he loved her? Well, did he? He wasn't sure, but he was fond enough of her not to lie, so he said what he could truthfully say. "I think you're super."

She smiled wryly at the word. She had never used it before, but she tried it out now to feel the sound of it on her lips. "Super . . . I've never thought of myself as super." She turned to face him at last.

"You ought to think of yourself that way," he said, taking her hand.

"Oh, Cliff," she whispered, her voice choking with gratitude and affection. "It was you who made me feel good about myself again . . . super—that's a good word for it . . . till now, that is. Now I feel very badly. I'm so ashamed of myself now . . ."

Cliff didn't understand. What could have made her feelings change so suddenly? Could she really have changed her mind about J.R. so quickly? And about him? And if she had, why had she?

Seeing his perplexity, she moved to relieve him

of it. "You see, Cliff, everything's changed since yesterday. I'm going to have a baby."

Cliff blinked, as if what he had just heard had to be part of a dream, but the reality was still there. It was no dream. "A baby!" he cried. "What do you mean? Do you mean to say you're pregnant?"

"That's right, Cliff," she said.

He stood there stunned as it slowly dawned on him what had happened, what must have happened. Then he burst out laughing.

"What in the world is so funny?" Sue Ellen asked him, somewhat miffed. Of all the reactions she had anticipated, laughter was certainly not one of them. She wondered how he could care for her as much as he professed to and still find it all so amusing.

Cliff quickly stifled his laughter, waving his hand as if to say, you don't understand. "No, what it is," he explained, "is just that you've been trying with J.R. for what is it, seven years or so? And in all that time, you couldn't get pregnant. But after just six weeks with me, bang!"

She stood there, shocked by the smug smile on his face. As far as she was concerned he was being incredibly crass. Didn't he understand what this meant to her? To them? "Cliff, is that all I mean to you? A way to get back at J.R., to humiliate him? Is this just some kind of potency contest in your mind? Because if it is, Cliff, I don't think you ought to be so self-assured. It could be J.R.'s baby, too, you know."

Cliff laughed and shook his head in disbelief. "Sue Ellen, after all you've told me, I don't know how you can say that. That baby has to be mine."

Sue Ellen's nostrils flared defiantly. "That's not

true, Cliff. There's at least some chance that it's J.R.'s baby. We may not touch each other very often, but we are married nevertheless."

"Come off it, Sue Ellen," he drawled. "What are the odds, do you think? Ten to one? Fifty to one? Whatever the odds, it sure is a long shot."

"Even so," she shot back at him, "say it is J.R.'s. What then?"

Cliff thought about this for a moment, then shrugged complacently. "Wouldn't really make any difference at all, as far as I can tell."

Now Sue Ellen was really confused. She felt that she was looking at a total stranger whose thoughts and feelings were completely new to her and whom she wasn't sure she liked. What did he mean, there wasn't any difference?

He answered her unspoken question. "You see," he said, his hand on her shoulder, "that baby could be mine, or it could be J.R.'s, or it could be Joe Shmo's . . . but whoever's baby it happens to be, you aren't going to be going anywhere fast. You're going to stay at Southfork with J.R. and all his money and power and prestige. There's no way you'd leave all that for poor old Cliff Barnes. Not now. Not ever."

Sue Ellen's lip trembled, struck by the hard blow of the truth. "If it hadn't been for the baby, I might have left him and come to you," she said plaintively. In spite of the way his remark had shaken her, she still believed it was true.

Cliff, however, remained firm in his conviction. "Let me say something to you, Sue Ellen," he said gently, "something that may be difficult for you to hear, but believe me, it's the truth. We've always tried to be honest with each other, right from the start, at least as much as we could be, and I'm going to be perfectly honest with you now. You may have felt very strongly for me, even loved me. You may still, or at least you may think you do. But from the very beginning I knew there was no real chance for the two of us to make it. You weren't about to give up everything you have, to throw it all away just for this relationship. Not even before you knew you were pregnant. And now that you're carrying the heir to the Ewing kingdom, there's just no chance at all. Your stock is way up now over at the ranch, and you're not going to trade it in. You're too smart to do something rash like that."

There was a long silence as his words sunk in. She had had a dream, a beautiful dream. She was Juliet and Cliff was Romeo, and their star-crossed romance had been so beautiful . . . but the truth had come upon her with the force of a tidal wave, and the dream was drowning. "I guess, then, that it's over. Is it over, Cliff?"

He nodded sadly. "I'm afraid it is, Sue Ellen, much as it pains me to say it. I am very fond of you, you know . . . really I am. I'm not just saying that—I'm sure you know I mean it. And damn it all, aside from everything, I'm really happy about this. For you and for me both."

Sue Ellen did not understand.

"You see," Cliff explained, "it's like this. You're gonna have a baby, and that baby is going to inherit the Ewing Empire. Except that baby is probably not a Ewing at all, but a Barnes. A Barnes at the helm of Ewing Oil. Wouldn't that be cosmic justice!"

Jock and Ellie were waiting at the front door when

the taxi pulled up with their eldest son, the future proud papa. Dragging his suitcase after him, he paid the driver and headed for the house and into the open arms of his waiting parents who were beaming at him proudly.

"Oh, J.R., isn't it wonderful! I'm so pleased," said his mother.

"Me too, Momma," replied J.R. "I'm pleased as punch." But he was already looking over at his father, whose love was the richest prize in the world to him, to see what his reaction was.

Jock was aglow with pride and happiness, and J.R. felt as if God had touched him with grace.

"Hello, Daddy," he said shyly. He put his hand out for Jock to shake, but instead his father grabbed it and pulled him into a warm bear hug.

"J.R., I'm proud of you, son. It's about time."

"I appreciate it, Daddy. I'm glad you're happy."

Jock released him, holding him out in front of him so he could get a good look at him. "I'll tell you something, boy," he said sternly. "For a long time I've thought you were never going to give me a grandchild. My oldest son, finally a father . . . it feels good . . . it feels real good."

J.R. felt his eyes misting over with sentimental tears, and he had to beat them back. "You know, Daddy . . . Momma, all the way home on the plane I kept thinking of the two of you and how pleased I knew you'd be. All I want is to make you happy and proud of me."

Ellie beamed. "We are, J.R. This is the most wonderful thing that's happened in this family in a long, long time."

The greetings done, J.R. looked around and noticed that the three of them were alone. No one else in the family, apparently, had thought it fit to come out and greet the triumphant returning hero. It irked him quite a bit, and it was hard for him to sound casual. "Everybody off someplace? Where's Sue Ellen? Didn't she know I was coming?"

Ellie ran off everybody on her fingers for him. "Let's see, Lucy's at school of course, and Bobby and Pam are still out at work . . . Sue Ellen's gone into town. She had an appointment with the doctor."

J.R.'s face darkened. "There's nothing wrong with her is there?" he said, alarmed.

"No, no," Jock boomed, amused at his son's sudden and unaccustomed concern for his wife's welfare. How quickly feelings can change, he was thinking. "Just a regular check-up, she said. She ought to be back anytime . . . nothing to worry about, son." Throwing his arm once again around his son's shoulder, he said, "Hey, boy! Let's go inside—I'm feeling mighty generous this afternoon. How 'bout if I buy you a drink?" Laughing and smiling, the two men walked into the house.

Ellie gazed after them, her face aglow with happiness. This was the way she had always wanted it to happen . . . this was what they had all been waiting for. Everything would be all right now, she was sure of it.

Pam hung up the phone, and, turning to the mirror, began brushing her hair. She looked herself up and down. Even she had to admit she looked terrific. And she felt terrific, too. She knew, she felt absolutely sure, that she had done what she had to do. Whether it was right or not she could not say, but she knew that it was right for her. Bobby entered quietly with a big box under his arm, and she immediately saw his figure outlined in the mirror.

"Hello there," she said, startling him.

He had thought he was entering unobserved. "Hello," he replied. "Sorry it took me so long to get here."

"Have you gotten a load of J.R. since he got back?" she asked him.

"Oh, yeah. The last time he had a smile that big on his face was when the Arabs jacked up the price of oil by 500%."

They laughed, full of affection for one another, and for themselves, too.

Pam wanted to tell Bobby everything. It had taken her such a long time, but now she was ready. "Can I talk to you Bobby?" she asked. "It'll only take a minute, but it's very important."

"Okay," he replied, "but first I want to give you this." He thrust the box forward into her hands.

Opening it, she discovered a slinky, elegant full-length dress. She held it up in front of her. It was magnificent, and she could tell it would look smashing on her. "My God, Bobby—it's beautiful! What did I do to deserve this?"

"Well," he replied, a twinkle in his eye, "I didn't want my wife going to Paris in just anything."

It took a moment for his words to sink in. Then, a great rush of affection for this prince of a man she had married washed over her. "You knew about it!" she cried. He nodded confirmation. "Oh, Bobby, do you know how much I love you?"

"I know everything, Pam—haven't you learned that by now?" he quipped.

"I'm not so sure you do know everything." She smiled.

"Try me," he challenged her.

"For instance, you were right that I would be needing a dress to wear, but I'll be wearing it right here at Southfork—at your big party."

Now it was Bobby's turn to be confused—how could she be in two places at the same time?

"I've decided to pass up the trip to Paris," she explained.

"Oh?" he said, caught up short by her startling admission. "What do you mean, you're not going? I don't understand."

"I just now happened to get off the phone with Liz Craig," she said. "I called to tell her that although I love my work and it means a great deal to me, you mean even more. You're the most important thing in my life, Bobby—there are always other jobs, but never another Bobby Ewing."

They moved into each other's arms. Like in the old story, they had sacrificed their most heartfelt dreams for their love for each other. They had given each other the most precious gift they could give—themselves. More in love than ever before, their relationship was more solid with each passing moment. They gazed into each other's eyes, overcome with love.

"So what happened?" he asked her. "Did you lose your job?"

She shook her head happily. "Liz was pretty upset, but I was great, Bobby—you should have heard me. By the time I hung up I had her admitting that she would have done the same thing if she'd had you for a husband!"

Bobby laughed out loud. "You ought to be a salesman, not a buyer!" he said, as he kissed her long and deeply, and they sank down onto the bed in rapturous passion, celebrating their love with the embrace of ecstasy.

J.R. and Sue Ellen stood face to face, alone in the den. It was late at night, and the rest of the family had retired to their rooms. They held champagne glasses in their hands, and J.R. was pouring them each another glass from a bottle that was now practically empty. Once again, for the third or fourth time, he raised his glass and toasted, "To us, to you, and to the baby!"

"Thank you, sweetheart," she whispered.

Putting the bottle back on the bar, he came back and sat down next to her on the sofa. There was something gnawing at the back of his mind, something that had been bothering him almost from the time he had heard the news.

"Darlin'," he began, getting comfortable, his arm around her affectionately, "what was it that made you decide to go see the doctor for a pregnancy test?"

"Well," she replied, "that's not what I went in for, you see. I'd been feeling poorly, not able to get my food down, and I thought there must be something terribly wrong with me—I'd never felt like that before. I just called him up to get it diagnosed so I'd feel better."

"I see," said her husband, "and that was how it happened, huh? There's nothing else wrong with you? You feeling good now?"

"Oh, yes," she smiled, "just super."

Super. It was a word he had never heard her use

before. Where had she gotten hold of it? "Well," he said, "tell me everything, from the very beginning. How many weeks pregnant are you?"

"Um . . ." she was hedging. "The doctor says almost six weeks . . . that's his best guess."

J.R. took his arm from around her shoulder and brought it to his mouth. "Six weeks . ." he repeated softly to himself. "Isn't that something . . . six weeks ago was right about the time of Lucy's birthday party wasn't it?"

She shrugged, trying to seem casual. "I guess that's right . . ." she murmured.

"Well darlin'," he said, a hard edge creeping into his voice as he turned to face her, "are you positive it's not any farther along than that?"

"Not positive, J.R.," she said, fear in her eyes. "Why do you ask?"

"I ask because—" he said darkly, "I don't see how it's possible for you to be six weeks pregnant, Sue Ellen."

She looked at him questioningly, pretending not to catch his drift, hoping his meaning was not what she thought it was.

"I'm thinking back now, and I'm thinking real hard, and I don't believe we've touched each other for a good deal longer than six weeks. I don't see how we could have conceived a child as recently as six weeks ago. And now that I think of it," he continued, his voice rising to an angry crescendo, "didn't I take that ten-day junket to Austin six weeks ago? Yes, I did! So how in the hell can you be six weeks pregnant, Sue Ellen?"

Sue Ellen's face took on an expression of contempt. She had an ace in the hole, and she was now going to play it. "In spite of the fact that you touch me so rarely, once in a blue moon the impossible does happen. And, as you seem to have forgotten, you did come back from Austin for the weekend. It's amazing that such a rare event seems to have slipped your mind. I was sure you'd remember it. Is it possible you've forgotten?"

J.R. fell silent for a moment as he searched his memory in vain for that lost weekend. Then he shook himself. "Look, Sue Ellen—no matter what you say, something doesn't make sense about all this. Let's say I did remember that weekend, which I don't—even if it's true, don't you think it's mighty odd that after seven years of drought, all it would take would be one night to get you pregnant?"

"Well, J.R.," she replied, "whenever it happens, it's always in one night, isn't it? And besides, I've heard stranger stories than that. They do happen, you know."

"Not to J.R. Ewing they don't," he insisted.

"Why don't you just come right out and say it, J.R.? I know what you're thinking—that you're not the father of my child! You'd never dare suggest it, would you? It would be too humiliating for you, wouldn't it? All right, I'll ask it for you—are you the father of my child?"

He stared at her, his eyes shooting daggers. "Well?" he prompted her.

"Let me put it this way, darlin'," she said venomously, taking pleasure in the moment of power over him, "I have been just as faithful to you as you have been to me."

J.R. sucked in his breath with a hiss. The full impact of her words hit him like the blow of a hammer. He knew that she knew about his deceptions. A man, after all, is entitled to his little flings; it's only natural. But a woman on the other hand . . . and now she was telling him she had cheated on him! He was as close as he could come to killing her, but he sat there. He had to. She kept talking, driving the knife deeper and deeper into him.

"All you really care about is the baby, anyway. Isn't that right, J.R.? I could go hang, as far as you're concerned. But I've got the baby now. The Ewing heir . . . more precious than diamonds. And guess what? You're gonna be very nice to me from now on . . . whether this baby is yours or not!"

Crack! His hand whipped across her cheek, and the slap resounded through the empty room.

Sue Ellen smiled. She knew that for the first time since she had married him, she had the upper hand with J.R. And she was going to use it. "You will never do that to me again, J.R. Do you understand?"

"Don't you tell me what I can and cannot do—" he began.

But she cut him off with a wave of her hand. "Oh no you won't," she hissed at him. "You can't. I'm carrying our baby, remember?"

"*Our* baby?" he repeated, his words tasting bitter in his mouth, as all his happiness turned to gall.

"It probably is, J.R. And what if it's not yours, what are you going to do? Run and tell Jock that it isn't yours? That you let your wife step out on you? I wonder what he'd think of your masculinity then, J.R.! And how about all the boys at the club? What would they think of you? You'd be the butt of jokes for the rest of your life!"

J.R. sat there stunned into silence as the horrible truth of what she was saying sank in. He was caught and he knew it.

"This is something you're gonna have to get used to, J.R.," Sue Ellen was saying, still rubbing it in. All the anger of seven years was coming to the surface in one great wave of fury. "Look on the bright side, darlin'—it might be yours, after all."

So. It was going to be war. J.R. sat there, silently taking it all in. He knew he had lost the first battle—a surprise attack when his guard was down. But he was a very resourceful man, and he would find a way to emerge the victor. He always did. The war had just begun.

Gaze into the
"Soap Opera future"
with

Special Offer!

Soaps Exclusive is the weekly
newsletter that keeps you informed and
up-to-date on all the shows—never
again will you miss that all-important
crucial episode.

Soaps Exclusive enables you to amaze
your friends with accurate predictions of
events to come. Every single day of the
week, every week of the year, one week
in advance, you'll see the future as is
reported in the pages of *Soaps Exclusive*.

● Day by day
sneak previews of
all soap operas.

● All the action
before it happens,
alerting you to
episodes you won't
want to miss.

● Exclusive inside
story information
revealed as it is
happening.

Please start my subscription to your weekly newsletter,
Soaps Exclusive, immediately. I have enclosed a check or
money order.

☐ $15 for
13 weeks

☐ $26 for
26 weeks

☐ $50 for
52 weeks

Name (Print)

Address

City   State   Zip

Telephone (optional) (   )
                        area code

Send to:

Soaps Exclusive **1638 New Highway, Farmingdale, NY 11735**

(This is a special, limited offer and may be withdrawn at any time.)

Special Limited Offer to Soaps & Serials™ Readers!

**ONLY
$7.95!**
plus Shipping
& Handling

**SAVE
25%!**

The GIANT History Book of
DALLAS™

★ Relive the excitement of the complete Ewing Family Saga!
★ Hundreds of wonderful photos — many in full color!
★ *Special Discount* for Soaps & Serials™ readers! Save 25% off the cover price!

★ A unique collector's item for every *Dallas™* fan!
★ More than 200 pages filled with the adventures of *J.R., Bobby, Miss Ellie, Jock, Sue Ellen, Pamela* and all your favorite characters!
★ Published by Doubleday/Dolphin

– –

To get your copy of DALLAS,™ mail this coupon along with your check or money order for $9.90 (price includes $1.95 for shipping & handling) to: Soaps & Serials™, P.O. Box 5006, Rocky Hill, CT 06067.

Name _____

Street _____ Apt. No. _____

City _____ State _____ Zip _____

Telephone (area code)_____

Dallas TM & © 1986 Lorimar Productions, Inc. All Rights Reserved.
Soaps & Serials TM & © 1986. Pioneer Communications Network, Inc. All rights reserved.

Yes!

TRIPLE BONUS COUPON

SUBSCRIBE NOW!!
We're out to make YOU a WINNER!!

Mail to:
TV Game Show Magazine
P.O. Box 856, Farmingdale, N.Y. 11737

☐ **Send me 12 + 2 issues for just $19.95.** I'm saving
27% off the newsstand price. **Plus a $3.95 book FREE.**

☐ Check enclosed   ☐ Money Order enclosed

Charge My Credit Card: ☐ **MASTERCARD**   ☐ **VISA**

Signature X _____

CARD #: _____   EXPIRES: _____

NAME _____
           (please print)

ADDRESS _____

CITY _____   STATE _____   ZIP _____

Please allow 6 to 8 weeks for delivery.

769219

How to Win Big Prizes

tv game show MAGAZINE ®

GET 2 ISSUES FREE

SAVE $7.35

America's only TV Game Show Magazine **has it all!!!**

- All the TV Game Shows
- All your Favorite Stars
- How to get on TV
- Secrets of TV game show stars

- Read what television won't show you
- Personal, revealing interviews
- All Winners

- Read about Pat Sajak, Wink Martindale, Bob Eubanks, Vanna White, Richard Dawson and many more
- Photos, Gossip

And Much More!!

ENCYCLOPEDIA

- Gamshows on Networks, Cable & Local TV
- Host Names & Contacts
- Studio Addresses
- Producer Names & Contacts
- Reviews
- Prizes

tv game show

+ This Book FREE

Subscription details on reverse side

A SPECIAL OFFER

For Parents of Children in grades 2 through 5

WRITE•ABOUT
by Judith Pasamanick, Ph. D.

Schools now spend $14.95 to purchase **WRITE•ABOUT** for their students. But as a reader of Soaps & Serials, you can obtain **WRITE•ABOUT** for just $9.95 (plus shipping and handling).

And here's what you'll get: over 300 pages chock full of imaginative, fun-filled activities for your child. **WRITE•ABOUT** gets your child started with his or her own diary, drawing on personal experiences, thoughts, and feelings. It goes on to introduce fables, tall-tales, metaphors, novels, drama, and narrative and descriptive writing, and more, much more. **WRITE•ABOUT** provides hours and hours of activities—stories, poems, songs and riddles.

WRITE•ABOUT was a major selection of the Early Learning Book Club, the Teacher Book Club and the Library of Special Education.

Please send me **WRITE•ABOUT**. I enclose $11.95 ($9.95 plus $2.00 for shipping and handling) for each set.

Name _____

Address _____

City _____ State _____ Zip _____

If not satisfied, I may return in 10 days for a full refund.

Send to: Center for Media Development, Inc.
Dept. SS, Box 51, Great Neck, N.Y. 11021

Only from Pioneer Communications Network, Inc.

OVER 5 MILLION BOOKS IN PRINT!